"Chuck Black is a word crafter who is able to weave Kingdom principles into the fabric of one's moral imagination. The characters he has created and the passions they exude will motivate readers to follow their examples, which have now been etched into their awakened conscience."

—MARK HAMBY, founder and president of Cornerstone
Family Ministries and Lamplighter Publishing

"With sanctified imagination, Chuck Black transports readers back to the days of chivalry and valor, clashing steel and noble conflict—but ultimately he transports readers to the eternal triumph of the King who reigns!"

—DOUGLAS BOND, author of *Hold Fast in a Broken World*
and *Guns of the Lion*

"My son, Nathan, loved the first book in the series, and he said the second was even better. In my son's own words, 'Mom, it was exciting and full of mystery. It compelled me to read more. I couldn't put it down.' As a mom and an author, I give *Sir Bentley and Holbrook Court* two thumbs up!"

—TRICIA GOYER, homeschooling mom and author
of *Blue Like Play Dough*

"Chuck Black is the John Bunyan of our times! *Sir Kendrick and the Castle of Bel Lione* is a reminder of the origins of the spiritual warfare we are to fight daily."

—IACI FLANDERS, inductive Bible study teacher
and homeschooling mom

ALSO BY CHUCK BLACK

THE KINGDOM SERIES
Kingdom's Dawn (Book One)
Kingdom's Hope (Book Two)
Kingdom's Edge (Book Three)
Kingdom's Call (Book Four)
Kingdom's Quest (Book Five)
Kingdom's Reign (Book Six)

THE KNIGHTS OF ARRETHTRAE SERIES
Sir Kendrick and the Castle of Bel Lione (Book One)
Sir Bentley and Holbrook Court (Book Two)
Sir Dalton and the Shadow Heart (Book Three)
Lady Carliss and the Waters of Moorue (Book Four)
Sir Quinlan and the Swords of Valor (Book Five)

SIR ROWAN

AND THE CAMERIAN CONQUEST

CHUCK BLACK

MULTNOMAH
BOOKS

SIR ROWAN AND THE CAMERIAN CONQUEST
PUBLISHED BY MULTNOMAH BOOKS
12265 Oracle Boulevard, Suite 200
Colorado Springs, Colorado 80921

Scripture quotations and paraphrases, unless otherwise indicated, are taken from the New King James Version®. Copyright © 1982 by Thomas Nelson Inc. Used by permission. All rights reserved. Scripture quotations marked (KJV) are taken from the King James Version.

The characters and events in this book are fictional, and any resemblance to actual persons or events is coincidental.

ISBN 978-1-60142-129-6
ISBN 978-1-60142-296-5 (electronic)

Published in the United States by WaterBrook Multnomah, an imprint of the Crown Publishing Group, a division of Random House Inc., New York.

MULTNOMAH and its mountain colophon are registered trademarks of Random House Inc.

Library of Congress Cataloging-in-Publication Data
Black, Chuck.
    Sir Rowan and the Camerian conquest / Chuck Black ; [illustrations by Marcella Johnson]. — 1st ed.
        p. cm.
    Summary: Knights Rowan and Lijah battle enemies of the King and, when they ultimately come face to face with the Dark Knight in disguise, must do battle to save the United Cities of Cameria from total destruction.
    ISBN 978-1-60142-129-6 — ISBN 978-1-60142-296-5 (electronic)
    [1. Knights and knighthood—Fiction. 2. Good and evil—Fiction. 3. Christian life—Fiction. 4. Allegories.] I. Johnson, Marcella, ill. II. Title.
    PZ7.B528676Skt 2010
    [Fic]—dc22

                                2010019203

Printed in the United States of America
2010—First Edition

10 9 8 7 6 5 4 3 2 1

♛ ♛ ♛

To my grandmother Izetta…
a faithful servant of the King who lived her life
as a testimony, bringing many to Christ

CONTENTS

Kingdom's Heart: An Introduction to the Knights of Arrethtrae 1

Prologue: Cameria the Great 4

Chapter 1: Stable Boy 6

Chapter 2: Bread and Tournaments 11

Chapter 3: The Victory Cloak 16

Chapter 4: The Grand Trophy Quest 21

Chapter 5: One Hundred to One 26

Chapter 6: Prison with No End 32

Chapter 7: Journey of Dreams 39

Chapter 8: A Song in the Dark 43

Chapter 9: Homeward Bound 48

Chapter 10: The Work of One 56

Chapter 11: Mysterious Knight 62

Chapter 12: Bandits 67

Chapter 13: The Resolutes 74

Chapter 14: Flight of the Eagle 82

Chapter 15: Higher Calling 90

Chapter 16: The Battle for Laos 101

Chapter 17: The Conquest of Cameria 109

Chapter 18: A Hopeless Fight 119

Chapter 19: Call of the Prince 125

Chapter 20: The Armor of the King 132

Chapter 21: Chessington's Promise 138

Chapter 22: The Final Stand 146

Chapter 23: Life Like the Prince 155

Epilogue: Across the Great Sea 159

Discussion Questions 161

Answers to Discussion Questions 169

"The Final Call"
    (written for *Sir Rowan and the Camerian Conquest*) 176

Author Commentary 181

KINGDOM'S HEART

An Introduction to the Knights of Arrethtrae

Like raindrops on a still summer's eve, the words of a story can oft fall grayly upon the ears of a disinterested soul. I am Cedric of Chessington, humble servant of the Prince, and should my inadequate telling of the tales of these brave knights e'er sound as such, know that it is I who have failed and not the gallant hearts of those of whom I write, for their journeys into darkened lands to save the lives of hopeless people deserve a legacy I could never aspire to pen with appropriate skill. These men and women of princely mettle risked their very lives and endured the pounding of countless battles to deliver the message of hope and life to the far reaches of the kingdom of Arrethtrae…even to those regions over which Lucius, the Dark Knight, had gained complete dominion through the strongholds of his Shadow Warriors.

What is this hope they bring? To tell it requires another story, much of it chronicled upon previous parchments, yet worthy of much retelling.

Listen then to the tale of a great King who ruled the Kingdom Across the Sea, along with His Son and their gallant and mighty force of

Silent Warriors. A ruler of great power, justice, and mercy, this King sought to establish His rule in the land of Arrethtrae. To this end He chose a pure young man named Peyton and his wife, Dinan, to govern the land.

All was well in Arrethtrae until the rebellion…for there came a time when the King's first and most powerful Silent Warrior, Lucius by name, drew a third of the warriors with him in an attempt to overthrow the kingdom. A great battle raged in the Kingdom Across the Sea until finally the King's forces prevailed. Cast out of the kingdom—and consumed with hatred and revenge—Lucius now brought his rebellion to the land of Arrethtrae, overthrowing Peyton and Dinan and bringing great turmoil to the land.

But the King did not forget His people in Arrethtrae. He established the order of the Noble Knights to protect them until the day they would be delivered from the clutches of the Dark Knight. The great city of Chessington served as a tower of promise and hope in the darkened lands of Arrethtrae.

For many years and through great adversity, the Noble Knights persevered, waiting for the King's promised Deliverer.

Even the noblest of hearts can be corrupted, however, and long waiting can dim the brightest hope. Thus, through the years, the Noble Knights grew selfish and greedy. Worse, they forgot the very nature of their charge. For when the King sent His only Son, the Prince, to prepare His people for battle against Lucius, the Noble Knights knew Him not, nor did they heed His call to arms.

When He rebuked their selfish ways, they mocked and disregarded Him. When He began to train a force of commoners—for He was a true master of the sword—they plotted against Him. Then the Noble Knights, claiming to act in the great King's name, captured and killed His very own Son.

What a dark day that was! Lucius and his evil minions—now known as Shadow Warriors—reveled in this apparent victory. But all was not lost. For when the hope of the kingdom seemed to vanish and the hearts of the humble despaired, the King used the power of the Life Spice to raise His Son from the dead.

This is a mysterious tale indeed, but a true one. For the Prince was seen by many before He returned to His Father across the Great Sea. And to those who loved and followed Him—myself among them—He left a promise and a charge.

Here then is the promise: that the Prince will come again to take all who believe in Him home to the Kingdom Across the Sea.

And this is the charge: that those who love Him must travel to the far reaches of the kingdom of Arrethtrae, tell all people of Him and His imminent return, and wage war against Lucius and his Shadow Warriors.

Thus we wait in expectation. And while we wait, we fight against evil and battle to save the souls of many from darkness.

We are the knights who live and die in loyal service to the King and the Prince. Though not perfect in our call to royal duty, we know the power of the Prince resonates in our swords, and the rubble of a thousand strongholds testifies to our strength of heart and soul.

There are many warriors in this land of Arrethtrae, many knights who serve many masters. But the knights of whom I write are my brothers and sisters, the Knights of the Prince.

They are mighty because they serve a mighty King and His Son.

They are…the Knights of Arrethtrae!

CAMERIA THE GREAT

 In the days of the great war against Chessington, the Dark Knight nearly destroyed the King's people. They were scattered from one end of the kingdom to the other, and though many did not believe the Prince to be the true Son of the King, the King did not forget them nor His promise to them. Those who did believe, the Knights of the Prince, were likewise spread from coast to coast. Wherever they went, they took the truth of the Prince and made brothers and sisters of enemies and strangers.

It was during these days that brave knights carried the mission of the Prince across the vast expanse of the Altica Valley to the five cities of Cameria. At first the Dark Knight paid no heed to their seemingly feeble efforts, for he deemed this region too remote from Chessington to matter. But the Camerian cities embraced the truth of the Prince and grew strong in the ways of the Code. This truth united the five great cities, and Cameria grew to be one of the most powerful regions in all the kingdom.

Many great Knights of the Prince arose in Cameria to battle against the evil one—knights whose stories deserve their own telling in another book of chronicles. Their love for the King and His Son inspired the people of this great land to reach across the vastness of the Altica Valley and help the people of Chessington in their darkest hour. They bred horses that could endure the harsh travel required, and they flew across the valley as if on the wings of eagles. And it was they who gave battle against one of Lucius's most formidable Vincero Knights, Sir Adophal, who had risen up to conquer much of the southern kingdom. When this vile knight had nearly destroyed all that was Chessington, when the Dark Knight was ready to proclaim himself king of all Arrethtrae, the United Cities of Cameria came to the rescue of the King's people.

They snatched victory from the jaws of the great dragon, inspiring the dragon's terrible wrath against Cameria and its people. But the truth of the Prince was so strong in Cameria and its Knights of the Prince so wary of the dragon that the Dark Knight could not overcome them by force. So he turned to more subtle tactics, scheming to infiltrate Cameria with thousands of Shadow Warriors and Vincero Knights and destroy the people and their great cities from within. The victory would be accomplished not by might but by deception, apathy, and entertainment.

As the years passed, the Dark Knight waited patiently for his evil scheme to take effect. Slowly, as a weed grows up beside the wheat stem, the deceptions of the Dark Knight began to choke the once-vibrant truth of the Prince from the hearts of the Camerians.

Gradually they forgot the Prince.

Then they forgot Chessington…and the Dark Knight claimed victory.

With his heart overflowing with hatred, the Dark Knight then turned his eyes once more to Chessington and resumed his war against the King's people—a war that would rage on until the great day of the Prince's return.

For a time, however, the Camerians delayed the evil hand of Lucius, the Dark Knight. Some might think that the tale of their conquest is a tragedy, but out of every tragedy rise heroes—heroes whose chronicles are worth telling.

This is the story of such a one…the story of Sir Rowan.

ONE

STABLE BOY

Some men are born to be poets, some to be builders, others bakers, sheriffs, and stable masters. But Rowan of Laos was born to be a swordsman, and every fiber of his body seemed to know it. His mastery of the art form was as instinctual as an eagle's drive to soar in the seam of sky between the mountain peaks and the blue canvas above them. And though he was born in utter poverty and orphaned at an age too early to remember his parents, something deep within him always whispered that he was destined for greatness.

As a boy, Rowan watched knights duel in the tournaments of Laos, memorizing every stance and move that he and the other boys of the street could practice later with their makeshift wooden swords. By age twelve, though he'd never held a real sword, he knew every move of the great fighters—knights like Sir Tarrington, Sir Byrk, Sir Borlan, and Sir Padruth.

Rowan loved sword fighting with a mighty passion, yet his chances of ever owning a sword were slim to none. He barely managed to eat, surviving on the handouts of passersby. As he grew, he eventually found work in one of the city stables, which provided some food and a reasonably dry place to sleep. Though he yearned to be a gallant knight someday and fight in the tournaments, his poverty gave him no hope of becoming anything more than a stable boy.

It was a fine horse named Algonquin that finally gave young Rowan of Laos his chance. Rowan was tacking up the stallion on a cool spring morning when Algonquin's owner came to collect his steed.

"He's a fine animal, sir." Rowan handed the reins over to a tall knight with dark brown eyes and a friendly face, then swiped a tousle of blond hair from his eyes and wiped a sleeve across his nose.

Sir Aldwyn smiled. "Thank you. Looks like you've taken good care of him. Here—" He pressed a coin into Rowan's hand, then winked.

Rowan's face lit up. "Thank you, sir." He eyed the coin as though he'd been given the world. Then his smile slowly disappeared.

Aldwyn tilted his head at the strange response.

"What is it, boy?" he asked.

Rowan glanced at the splendid sword that hung from Sir Aldwyn's belt, then looked up at the knight.

"I'd…like to buy something from you, sir." Rowan's gaze went back to the sword that sparkled in the morning sun, its pommel brilliantly flashing a unique mark he had seen once before.

Sir Aldwyn's hand fell on the golden hilt of the sword as he followed Rowan's gaze. He placed a gentle hand on the lad's shoulder. "I'm afraid a sword such as this costs far more than you have."

Rowan looked up, his face flushed. "I…I know, for this *is* all I have. I don't want to buy it, sir." He swallowed hard, hesitating even to ask such a daring question of a knight. "May I buy a chance to hold it for just a moment?"

Sir Aldwyn stared hard at Rowan, stunned at the request. Rowan ducked his head and lowered his gaze. He slowly tucked the coin into a pocket and began to turn away. But the beautiful sound of steel sliding on steel touched his ears as Sir Aldwyn slowly removed his sword from the scabbard.

Rowan lifted his head, turned about, and watched with widened eyes as the slender silver blade made its final exit from its home. Sir Aldwyn held the sword across both hands, palms open, and offered it to Rowan. Rowan looked up with absolute hope in his eyes and caught the subtle nod of the knight.

His hands quivered as he reached out and touched first the perfect steel of the blade and then the intricate yet sturdy hilt that bore the load of such a gallant weapon. Slowly his right hand encircled the grip, and he lifted the weapon.

The sword felt good—no, it felt great—in his hands, almost as if he'd been reunited with a lost brother. It was weighty, but not as heavy as he'd expected. He held it before himself, wanting to take position and execute a cut. He glanced up at Sir Aldwyn. The knight nodded and stepped back. Rowan assumed a perfect middle-guard stance, then attacked an invisible enemy with a high to low diagonal cut followed by a horizontal cut and a quick thrust.

He held his final position, and chills flowed from the sword through his arms and up and down his entire body. He closed his eyes, trying to memorize the feel of the weapon in his hands. He relaxed, stood straight, and handed back the sword hilt first, the blade supported by his left hand, just as he'd seen the tournament chancellor do many times.

Sir Aldwyn took the sword and held it just a moment longer as Rowan soaked it up with his gaze, then placed it back in the scabbard. Rowan retrieved the coin from his pocket and held it out to Sir Aldwyn. The knight reached for it but instead closed Rowan's fingers around the coin.

"You have good form for such a young lad," Aldwyn said with a gaze that seemed to penetrate into Rowan's heart. "Come to the haven of the Prince, and I shall teach you."

He picked up Algonquin's reins, wheeled the horse around, and mounted. Rowan stood motionless, staring after him until he disappeared around the corner. Then he sprang to life and sprinted back into the stable to gather his meager belongings.

That was the day that changed Rowan's life forever. Sir Aldwyn mentored Rowan for the next four years, teaching him the ways of the Prince, the Code, and the sword. Rowan thrived under the training— fully embracing the truth of the Prince and the Code, at least at first.

Truth be told, his interest in Sir Aldwyn's stories eventually waned, but he reveled in the swordsmanship. With proper food and exercise, his body grew into that which it was intended to be—a powerfully muscled physique. His strength was beyond that of normal men, even at the youthful age of seventeen, and he soon mastered and exceeded all that Sir Aldwyn taught him about the sword.

On the day of Rowan's commissioning, Sir Aldwyn presented him with a magnificent sword of the Prince and invited him to ride by his side on a mission for the Prince. But though Rowan was grateful for Sir Aldwyn's kindness, the ventures of ordinary knights held no interest for him. He was determined to fight in the tournaments, to be one of the famous knights that stood before ten thousand cheering spectators.

At age eighteen, and against Sir Aldwyn's counsel, Rowan entered his first tournament and lost in the initial round. He had allowed the spectacle of the event to distract and hinder him. Afterward, the taunts and jeers of the small crowd so humiliated him that he wondered why he had even tried. As he walked through the arena gate, his embarrassment slowly transformed to determination. He glanced back into the arena as the next combatants entered under the cheers of many, and he vowed never to lose another fight—no matter the cost.

From that day forward, Rowan threw himself into training with single-minded determination. He pushed his body and his mind, drilling long hours each day, sparring with any partner he could find. After six months of intense work, Rowan registered for a small tournament in Sanisco, a city not far from Laos.

When the flag of commencement dropped, Rowan became so focused and determined that the sound of the crowd melted to silence and the stadium faded from sight. All he saw or heard was the knight before him and the sword the man held. An intensity akin to fury filled his veins, and after just a few strokes the duel was over. When he released the battle to victory, the sights and sounds of the arena flooded in upon him like the rushing waves of the sea. It was a glorious feeling, and Rowan reveled in it.

By day's end, Rowan was the champion of the Sanisco tournament.

He received the gold medallion amidst the cheers of hundreds of spectators, and a new tournament hero was born. As Rowan stood on the platform, satisfaction settled deep in his soul, and yet he hungered for more.

More crowds. More cheering. More glory and gold.

That day was the making—and the eventual unmaking—of the mighty Sir Rowan. ▨

TWO

BREAD AND TOURNAMENTS

 Steely blue eyes glared from behind ringlets of sweat-soaked sandy hair. Rowan gripped his sword tightly as the fight paused just long enough for the two combatants to reset their positions and their minds. The riotous roar of the crowd, previously lost in the rush of battle, engulfed them once more in endless concussions of cheers and chants. The two men stepped slowly in a clockwise motion, anticipating their next engagement.

This fight this day was everything for Rowan. After eighteen months of tournament victories, he had finally been allowed to compete at the grand Laos tournament. Sir Tarrington was the undisputed champion of Laos, the third largest city in Cameria. If by some miracle Rowan could defeat him, his ranking among tournament fighters would escalate. This would mean regional recognition by the Camerian Tournament Council.

Cameria had elevated the tournament events to a kingdomwide competition that transcended the games of Thecia and rivaled the bloody events of the old days. After the five major cities of Cameria united and battled to bring an end to Sir Adophal's reign of terror in the southern kingdom, an era of prosperity, power, and peace had dawned, and the people needed something new for which to cheer.

They were cheering now, riotously, and the roar gave Rowan a surge of energy. He looked into Sir Tarrington's eyes and saw surprise in them—the champion had not expected this level of competition from such a young man. Three judges watched just out of sword's reach. Five nonfatal hits would end the fight, but so would one fatal hit. The tally was four to three in Tarrington's favor.

Rowan prepared as Tarrington exploded a powerful advance. Rowan held his ground, but not without apprehension. He knew he was stronger than Tarrington, but there was always the element of experience to contend with. This often was the reason for the defeat of a rising competitor. Rowan had nearly fallen to Sir Yalteran in the previous duel because of it. He was determined to overcome that disadvantage now.

Tarrington's sword flew faster than ever before, but Rowan caught every thrust and refused to give ground. Their dancing swords arced, cut, and sliced in an endless volley of mastery. Rowan slowly turned the advance of Tarrington into retreat as he gained control of the flow of the fight and increased its tempo. His sword flew with the fury of a vengeful adversary to find its mark. The frenzied crowd roared, sensing that Sir Tarrington's near-decade reign as the champion of Laos was in jeopardy.

Then Rowan saw his first real opportunity. A cut from the left had put Tarrington's sword too far outside his torso and left him unbalanced. Rowan took advantage of the opening. He countered with a diagonal cut, then began a quick thrust that would be nearly impossible for Tarrington to parry. Midway through the thrust, however, he realized Tarrington's left foot had shifted slightly back, a sign that the champion's "mistake" had really been a ploy. Rowan pulled short on his thrust and recovered just in time to block Tarrington's intended victory cut. This time Tarrington truly was out of position, for he had gambled that Rowan would fall for his trick.

With one quick, powerful cut to Tarrington's head, the fight was over. Tarrington fell to the ground. Rowan covered him and nearly followed with another cut, but all three judges held up their red flags, indicating the end of the fight. Tarrington's helmet was dented, and he was dazed but uninjured.

The arena exploded with cheers and applause—there was a new champion in Laos. It took Rowan a moment to fully comprehend what had just happened. He had defeated the legendary Sir Tarrington in the Laos arena. He had risen from city street urchin to tournament champion, and the people loved it!

He reached down and offered Tarrington a hand up, and the veteran knight accepted. When he gained his feet, both men removed their helmets.

Tarrington looked deep into Rowan's eyes, almost with a look of relief.

"This is yours now. Defend it well." Tarrington grabbed Rowan's arm and raised it into the air. The crowd doubled its cheering. Rowan looked to the seat where he had arranged for Sir Aldwyn to sit. His mentor was clapping too, but there was no smile on his lips.

Rowan's spirits sank, but only for an instant. He looked at the cheering crowd, and their roar of approval carried him on a buoyant wave of exhilaration. Surely this was what he was meant to do.

It seemed as if he was born for it.

On the ceremony stand, Lord Gavaah himself presented the tournament sword, medal, money, and the coveted victory cloak to Rowan. The man's very presence was an honor, for Lord Gavaah was the impetus behind the Camerian Tournament Council. It was he who provided the wealth and the savvy to organize the tournaments at Elttaes, Amion, Laos, and Berwick into the first regional league of structured tournaments. Lord Gavaah's brilliant Bread and Tournaments strategy—offering free bread to anyone who attended the games—had brought nearly instant fame and success to what had been a loosely structured and unprofitable activity.

Within two years, the council had taken tournament attendance to a near frenzied level of participation. Lord Gavaah's return on his initial investment of fifty thousand loaves of bread and four opulent stadiums had made him wealthy beyond measure, and his influence in Cameria was widespread.

Rowan didn't really care who or how or why the tournaments had gained such popularity. He just loved them…every part of them. At first he had convinced himself that participating would be an effective way to proclaim the Prince, but somewhere along the way his call to be a Knight of the Prince had faded into the background and the tournaments themselves had become his priority. Now he basked in the glory that came with being a champion.

As the opulent victory cloak fell upon his shoulders, cheers erupted from twenty thousand spectators, and Rowan felt like a king. The cloak was a symbol of a true champion, for only those knights who had prevailed in one of the five major city tournaments received one.

Rowan hefted the beautiful sword with the Camerian Tournament Council emblem engraved in the pommel. It felt even better than the Knights of the Prince sword he had used to rise this far. The balance was perfect. This would be his new tournament sword…a sword to be envied by all.

It was still early in the tournament season, and Rowan would have to defend his new title a dozen times, but his future looked bright. He would represent the great city of Laos at the Camerian Games in Kroywen in six months' time, an honor only a few had ever won. Rowan had every intention of becoming champion of all Cameria.

When the accolades faded, Lord Gavaah put an arm around Rowan's shoulder and walked with him toward the edge of the platform. He was a handsome man whose shrewd eyes were softened by a hearty demeanor and a ready smile. He was known for his voice, a smooth baritone that could ring throughout a stadium or purr through a contract negotiation.

"You have the makings of a great Camerian champion, son." Lord Gavaah grinned broadly. His black mustache and beard glistened in the afternoon sun.

"Thank you, Lord Gavaah. It was an honor to fight Sir Tarrington."

Gavaah clapped him on the back. "You did more than fight him, Sir Rowan. You beat him. And now you are in a position to become one of the greatest swordsmen in all of Arrethtrae."

Rowan beamed at the sound of that.

"You and the CTC have much to gain if we are smart about how we proceed," Lord Gavaah added. "That's why I'd like to help you."

He gestured to a man just a few paces away. The man stepped forward and bowed. "Mr. Balenteen at your service."

"Mr. Balenteen is a CTC agent," Gavaah said. "He will help you manage your affairs."

"Ah…what affairs?" Rowan asked as he looked at Lord Gavaah.

Gavaah smiled. "Well, there's your money, your time, and"— Gavaah raised a hand to gesture toward the edge of the platform—"your followers."

Rowan's eyes opened wide as hundreds of people began to shout excitedly.

"I've also arranged for a trainer to help keep you in shape for the next round of tournaments. Mr. Balenteen will arrange a meeting with Sir Hatfield tomorrow."

Lord Gavaah slapped Rowan on the back again. "Get ready to make your dreams come true, young knight." He turned about, his purple cloak swirling in the wake behind him.

THREE

THE VICTORY
CLOAK

 Mr. Balenteen was an irritating little man with a balding head and a short black mustache, but Rowan quickly saw the genius in his methods and came to rely heavily upon him over the next few months. The victory over Sir Tarrington had catapulted Rowan from a no-name tournament knight to a Camerian hero. His new status brought not only a whole new level of wealth and popularity but a dizzying schedule of appearances and high-level meetings.

Mr. Balenteen managed all of that, making sure that Rowan appeared where and when he was expected. He managed Rowan's finances, helping him negotiate the complications of sudden fame, even making arrangements for Rowan to purchase and furnish a large estate on the east side of the city. He also kept his eye out for any chance to promote Rowan's reputation—which is why Rowan now stood facing a long line of young men brandishing swords and shields.

As he had occasionally done before, Mr. Balenteen was offering money to squires to skirmish against Rowan for training purposes. It was great publicity for Rowan, since many relished the opportunity to fight against someone so famous, even if their chances of winning were nil. Additionally, the sum that Mr. Balenteen offered was enough to entice some of the better fighters into the arena with Rowan, giving him at least a small challenge from time to time. Rowan's trainer, Sir Hatfield, had never been fond of the idea and closely supervised each event.

The sky was blue and the sun hot. After a dozen duels and a dozen victories, Rowan took off his helmet and wiped the sweat from his brow.

Sir Hatfield raised his hand. "That's enough for today." He walked toward Rowan. The trainer was a bulky red-headed fellow who knew the sword well and had studied all of the great fighters, both past and present. He also had the tournament experience that Rowan lacked.

Groans of disappointment rose up from the fifteen men still waiting for their chance at the money and the fight.

"Come back tomorrow, and we'll give you another chance," Balenteen said with a smile as he shooed the men toward the arena exit.

Hatfield shot Balenteen a look of disgust, then motioned him over. "What are you doing, Balenteen?" Hatfield put his hands on his hips but continued before the smooth-talking agent could answer. "I've got some serious training yet to do with Rowan, and these little publicity antics of yours are getting in the way!"

"It's Rowan's fame that pays our wages," Balenteen shot back. "We *both* have jobs to do—"

Rowan shook his head and turned away so his amusement wouldn't show. Balenteen and Hatfield were each the best at their jobs, which is why they were always getting on each other's nerves. At first Rowan had tried to smooth out their relationship, but eventually he had realized the futility of it. Now he just laughed and walked away. Besides, he was eager to clean up and relax after his long day at the arena.

Rowan sheathed his sword and walked over to his knapsack, glancing once more toward Balenteen and Hatfield, who were deep in a heated discussion as they walked out through the arena gate. The tired knight flung his victory cloak about his shoulders and fastened the tie across his chest. Then he picked up his knapsack and turned to leave, but one of the training squires was facing him with helmet and visor in place and sword drawn.

"We're done today, bloke." Rowan tried to walk past the squire, but the man sidestepped to cut him off. "Come back tomorrow," Rowan said, perturbed by the man's rude refusal.

"I will fight you." The squire swung his sword before him.

Rowan could tell by the stance and inexperienced grip that the squire was only just beginning his training as a knight. This was one of those impertinent, ill-trained glory seekers Rowan hated to encounter.

"Look, chap, my agent is gone and so is the money." Rowan tried to step around the squire once more, but the sword did not drop, and he was intercepted again.

Rowan clenched his jaw and tried to keep his anger from getting the best of him, but the long day had worn his patience thin. He dropped his knapsack, threw back one side of the cloak over his left shoulder, and drew his sword, intending to disarm the insolent fool quickly so he could be on his way. He glared at the squire as he swung his sword in a flourish across the space between them. The squire shuffled nervously as he seemed to understand the foolishness of his actions.

"Do you really want to do this?" Rowan's voice conveyed his indignation.

The squire hesitated, looking as if he might turn and run, but then he attacked with a volley of poorly executed cuts and slices. Rowan resisted the temptation to laugh as he easily thwarted each cut, playing with his opponent as a cat would a captured mouse.

When the man's initial attack ceased, Rowan planned to execute a cut-thrust-bind maneuver to disarm the inexperienced squire and quickly end the fight. The cut nearly blasted the sword from the squire's hand, but somehow he held on to it. Then the thrust nearly found its mark in the man's chest, and Rowan had to pull up short to keep from impaling the imbecile. But at the last moment, the squire was able to deflect Rowan's sword to the right.

Now Rowan was in the perfect position to end the fight. He executed a disarming bind, but the squire's sword held, and in that small subtle moment of time Rowan felt something strange through the blade of his sword. He felt strength from the squire that had not been apparent earlier. Their blades locked motionlessly as Rowan peered into the darkened slit of the squire's helmet.

Rowan left the bind and reengaged. This time, the man's sword seemed to fly faster and stronger than before. Rowan's anger surged as he realized the man had played him. He increased the intensity of the duel, bringing powerful cuts and slices to the fight. Remarkably, the squire kept pace. He retreated some at first, but within just a few moments, he had adjusted and was matching Rowan's advance with a powerful defense.

Rowan's anger soon turned to shock, for he was now holding nothing back. The empty arena clanged with the ferocious volley of a full tournament duel. When Rowan's advance had expired and the squire was still standing solidly before him, he hesitated and lowered his sword.

"Who are you?" Rowan asked, winded by his attack.

The man whipped his sword in a circular motion and assumed a powerful swordsman's stance. He paused for just a moment, giving Rowan only enough time to recover from his stupor, then attacked.

For the first time in many months, Rowan found himself retreating without a counterattack plan. The sword of this man flew faster and stronger than that of any tournament knight he had ever faced. Rowan's fear rose as he slowly realized his life was in jeopardy. He focused completely on simply keeping the man's blade from penetrating his defense.

Then it happened. Cut, slice, thrust, deflect—one fraction of a moment too slow, and Rowan could not recover. The man's sword arced upward across Rowan's chest, tearing into his victory cloak and severing the tie that held it about his shoulders. The blade continued upward. Rowan winced and turned, just missing the cutting tip of the man's blade. The move put him off balance, and he knew it was over. There was nothing he could do to stop the final cut of this master's blade.

Rowan stumbled backward as his cloak fell to the ground where he had stood. The moment came and went, but Rowan did not die. He recovered to see that the man had ended his attack. Rowan's victory cloak lay on the ground between them, revealing a long gash across the royal cloth where the medals were pinned.

Rowan was too stunned to speak. What had just happened?

The man lifted his gaze from the cloak to Rowan, and Rowan felt the chill of fear race up and down his spine. No one had ever beaten him so soundly. Was this the next tournament champion of Cameria?

"Who are you?" Rowan asked again.

The man stared back in silence, then turned and walked toward another gate that led out of the arena. Rowan knelt down to his victory cloak and lifted it from the dirt and straw field of the arena. Slowly the shock and humiliation of the fight washed away, and a tide of anger began to burn. The Camerian Tournament Council did not give a second victory cloak to any fighter, not even the grand champion. Rowan ran his finger across the jagged cut in the fine cloth and let the anger settle deep into his bosom.

"Whoever you are," he said quietly, "I will face you again one day when I am prepared. You will pay." Rowan tightly clenched the cloak, making a fist. "I swear it!"

FOUR

THE GRAND TROPHY QUEST

 Rowan continued to win tournament after tournament. Not only did he become one of the most decorated knights in Cameria, but he also won unprecedented favor with the crowds, for his charisma, handsome looks, and humble beginning were the stuff of legends. From Elttaes to Kroywen to Berwick, Rowan won the hearts of the people everywhere.

On the eve of his journey to Kroywen to participate in the annual Camerian Games, Rowan received a visitor at his manor, Eastgate.

"You've lost your way, Rowan."

Sir Aldwyn stood on the terrace of Rowan's beautiful estate looking at the majestic Boundary Mountains. After a moment of silence, he turned to face the man he'd trained from childhood.

"How can you say such a thing, Sir Aldwyn?" Rowan stood with arms crossed, trying to hide his frustration at hearing such a remark. His massive arms bulged with muscle as he motioned around his beautiful home and pointed toward his display of medals and awards. "Look at what I have achieved!" he said. "I'm champion of Laos, and after the tournament I may be champion of Cameria. I should think you would be happy for me. After all, it was your training that got me here."

Aldwyn slowly walked to stand before Rowan.

"This is not where my training was intended to take you, Rowan. What of the Prince? Do you still serve Him?"

"Of course I do," Rowan rebutted.

"Really?" Aldwyn gazed deeply into Rowan's eyes. "When is the last time you told someone about Him?"

Rowan turned away from Aldwyn's hard stare.

"When is the last time you thought about the Code and desired to live by it?" Aldwyn asked as Rowan walked away in silence. "Cameria is changing, and there are troubling times ahead. Now is the time to live with purpose!"

Rowan stood still with his back to Aldwyn.

"You have won money and fame," Aldwyn said quietly, "yet all this is vanity."

Rowan snapped about, his mended victory cloak swirling around him.

"I have a good chance of becoming the champion of Cameria and winning the grand trophy at the Camerian Games in Kroywen. I was born to fight, Aldwyn. You of all people should know that."

"Then fight for something of worth," Aldwyn shot back, "not the superficial applause of bread seekers and pretty maidens."

"They don't come just for the bread anymore." Rowan grinned. "They come to see *me*. I am loved not just in Laos but across all of Cameria."

"They don't love you!" Aldwyn scoffed. "They love the entertainment you bring them. Lose a couple of fights, and you'll see just what they really think of you."

Rowan felt his cheeks begin to burn, and he clenched his fists to control his anger. "I will not be humiliated by you in my own manor. This conversation is over. Good day, Sir Aldwyn." Rowan whisked his cloak between them as he turned and walked to the banister of the terrace.

After a moment of silence, Rowan heard Aldwyn walk to the doorway, then stop.

"When I began to train you, I knew you were destined to do something great. This is not it!"

Aldwyn's footsteps echoed down the hallway that led to the front parlor. When Rowan heard the servant open and close the door behind Aldwyn, he turned back to the terrace view.

Rowan stared into the evening sky until the dark blue turned black. The sting of Aldwyn's words lingered, and he found it difficult to dismiss them. Not until he began to focus on the upcoming Camerian Games at Kroywen did he begin to feel better.

The next morning, Rowan, Balenteen, Hatfield, three supporting squires, and four guards left Laos before the first golden rays of sun peeked over the eastern edge of the Boundary Mountains. The morning mist rose from the standing waters in the nearby forest like curtains of the day opening for the world to see. As they passed through a low-lying area, the wake of their steeds caused the mist to swirl about them.

It was the mist that kept them from seeing the man at first.

As they approached the arched stone bridge that spanned the river, however, they began to make out a lone figure standing in the middle of it. There was nothing majestic or ominous about the man, but Rowan shuddered anyway. The ten men slowed, not because they could not pass on either side, but because it was obvious the man was challenging their passage. Besides this, their horses seemed to find it impossible to press on. Something about the man frightened them.

The man was fully armored, with his visor down. His hands rested on the hilt of his sword, its tip on the ground before him. Rowan's horse danced in agitation, matching Rowan's uneasiness. He knew what this meant.

"Move aside or be run over," the captain of the guards commanded.

"Captain," Rowan said without taking his eyes from the figure on the bridge, "I'll handle this." He dismounted.

"Don't be a fool," Balenteen said. "We don't have time to squander on some petty squire hoping for a shot at you."

"For once, I agree with Balenteen, Rowan," Hatfield said.

Rowan handed the reins of his steed to Hatfield. He hesitated as he looked up at his trainer.

"Is there a knight better than I with the sword?" he asked.

Hatfield looked perplexed but didn't hesitate. "You are the best I've ever seen."

Rowan took a deep breath. "Then this is something I must do."

He walked toward the lone figure on the bridge as the other nine men held back, spectators in a strange arena.

His boots clicked on the stones as he traversed the bridge and approached the stranger. The man didn't really look threatening, and Rowan wondered if this was indeed the one who had bested him at training months before…and cost him so many hours of sleep since then. With each step he took, anger grew within him. His victory cloak swirled with the receding mist, the corners snapping with each punctuated step.

When he was within three paces, he stopped. The challenging knight didn't move, and Rowan just stared at him for a long while.

"Are you here to stop me?" Rowan finally asked.

The knight slowly nodded.

"Why?" Rowan asked. "Who sent you?"

"Turn back," the mysterious knight said calmly, "or you will be destroyed."

Rowan nearly laughed. *Destroyed?* he thought. "Tell whoever sent you that I *will* compete in the games and I *will* be the champion of Cameria." With that, Rowan drew his sword. "And I *will* be rid of you!"

Rowan followed his last words with a powerful slice that the man seemed late in responding to. Halfway through the slice, he had not even moved from his standing guard position. At the last moment, however, the man snapped his sword from rest to a defensive position, and Rowan's blade struck immovable steel.

In that instant, all of Rowan's confidence fled from him. Something in him recognized that he was facing the ultimate warrior—impenetrable defense, frightening offense, unmovable and superior purpose.

He fought against the truth of his realization just the same and began a series of cuts and slices, holding absolutely nothing back. Every blow and cut was met perfectly. Rowan exhausted himself in an unending successions of cuts, slices, and thrusts, refusing to accept the fact that he could not best his silent opponent.

Finally, in desperation, he threw a descending diagonal cut, followed by a horizontal slice and a thrust to the man's chest. The knight deflected each one, then put a bind on Rowan's sword that locked their blades together. Rowan looked at the swords and realized that, with one quick move, the knight could leave the bind and plunge his sword into Rowan's unprotected abdomen. Hoping to equalize the threat, Rowan drew his long knife. But the knight grabbed Rowan's wrist and twisted his hand in such a way that Rowan's forearm and hand exploded in pain.

The knight forced the knife's blade down and close to Rowan's chin until he could feel the cold steel against his own neck. The harder he pushed back, the sharper the pain that shot down his wrist and arm. *How can this man control me so?* he wondered.

Just when Rowan thought his life was over, he felt the tie around his neck slice in two and his victory cloak fall away from his shoulders. At the same time, he heard horses galloping toward him and knew that Hatfield and the guards were coming.

Once again Rowan found himself face to helmet with this mysterious knight, his victory cloak at his feet. Perplexed and beaten, he didn't know whether to be angry, humbled, or fearful.

"You have lost your way." The knight spoke calmly, with no sign of effort. "Turn back."

The knight released his bind and his painful hold on Rowan's wrist. He stepped back, sheathed his sword, and turned to walk away. Just a few paces behind them, Rowan heard Hatfield and the guards draw their swords and dismount. He held up a hand to stop them.

"Who are you?" Rowan yelled. The knight walked away in silence until he was clear of the bridge, then turned toward the woods.

"Who are you?" Rowan yelled louder, but the man just disappeared into the mist of the forest. ▨

FIVE

ONE HUNDRED TO ONE

 The fight with the mystery knight left Rowan rattled, even more so than before. Was this a tactic by one of the champion knights he would face at the tournaments? If any of them were this good, he didn't have a chance. Yet something told him the mysterious knight was not a tournament contender.

Their party journeyed on, and Rowan rode in silence. Balenteen tried in his annoying way to lighten his spirits by talking about the grand tournament ahead, but the agent's efforts did not help.

"Shut your mouth, Balenteen," Hatfield finally said, much to Rowan's relief.

By late morning, they reached the Rock Forest, known for trees growing thickly among scattered boulders. The road twisted and turned to navigate through the rugged landscape.

"Once we get through the forest, we should make good time to Kroywen." Balenteen smiled, venturing one more attempt at lightening Rowan's mood. "We ought to be there before sundown this evening. I've made arrangements at the finest inn of the city."

Rowan just nodded. He didn't want to encourage the man too much, or he would never stop talking again.

They rounded a bend in the road to find two men working on a wagon that had toppled its heavy load of wood. One wheel was off the wagon, and the cut timber was strewn from one side of the road to the other.

"You imbeciles," Balenteen blurted out. "You're blocking the road!"

"Sorry, sir," one of the men said. "Wheel jus' fell off."

"You can get round over there." The other man pointed to the right side of the road, where there was just enough room to pass by single file, skirting the trees and boulders to the right.

Balenteen cursed and ordered the two leading guards to guide their entourage in that direction. Rowan followed Balenteen off the road, but as he passed the wagon, one of the men looked up at him and slapped his partner.

"Aye," he said, "that's Sir Rowan of Laos!"

The other man's eyes opened wide, and the two men ran to Rowan's horse. The animal spooked a bit, and Rowan halted his steed.

"Are y' truly Sir Rowan?" the second man asked with excitement in his voice. "The champion of Laos?"

"Yes, it is I." Rowan smiled down on the men. Their enthusiasm helped awaken him from his muddled self-pity and reminded him how good it felt to be on this side of the conversation. Without the fame of the tournaments, he could very well be one of these common laborers.

The men came closer. "We hope t' be at the games next week to cheer for ye."

Both men were standing just beside him, staring up in great admiration.

"We must keep moving, Sir Rowan," Balenteen turned on his horse to see what the extra delay was. "We must make the inn before—"

Balenteen's words were cut short by a deadly arrow that struck the nearest guard square in the chest. A look of terror filled his eyes as he doubled over and fell to the ground. Balenteen's eyes widened as another arrow pierced the second guard. Balenteen turned back to the road, kicking his steed into a full gallop.

Before Rowan could respond, he felt himself being dragged to the ground by the two men as chaos erupted around him. Rowan heard more arrows splitting the air, followed by screams and the neighs of frightened horses. Rowan hit the ground with a thud that nearly knocked the wind out of him. He glanced toward Hatfield and saw him draw his sword. Rowan reached for his own sword, but one of the laborers had pinned his right arm to the ground while the other scrambled to grab his left. Dozens of marauders emerged from the forest trees, and a group of them ran at Rowan with swords drawn.

Rowan screamed in anger and blasted a full-force fist into the temple of the man clutching his right hand. The man fell to the ground, unconscious. Rowan rolled away from the other man and set one knee solidly on the ground. The man dived for him, but Rowan smashed his fist into the man's chest. He heard bones crack, and the man collapsed in a heap. Rowan drew his sword and gained his feet just in time to engage the marauders.

Rowan was a tournament knight who had never fought in real battle, but the anger and frustration of the morning still seethed in his blood, and he was eager to release it on someone. The first marauder charged, and Rowan reacted instinctively. He parried and thrust, downing the man, then prepared for the next. He wasted no time with the superfluous actions of tournament play. Two attacked at once, and Rowan easily handled them both.

More men came at him until it seemed there were a hundred marauders, all trying to kill him. His sword flew not only with the speed and strength of a well-toned fighting machine but also with the fury of battle anger, something Rowan had never fully felt before. Fifteen men went down and ten more encircled him, hesitant to advance. Rowan knew he could beat them all and more, but suddenly the attack stopped.

"Drop your sword!" one of the marauders screamed.

Rowan jerked his head in the direction of the voice. The men surrounding Rowan parted to reveal three men holding a wounded Hatfield in their grip. One held a knife to his neck. Two squires lay dead at his feet, but the third was held by two more marauders. The look of fear in the lad's face shook Rowan. Besides this, three marauders with crossbows were aiming their arrows at Rowan's chest.

"Drop your sword now, or they will die!" the man holding the knife commanded. "And so will you!" A jagged scar ran from his left eyebrow down beneath a black eye patch and then halfway down his cheek.

Rowan looked about for the other two guards and spotted their lifeless bodies nearby. He was breathing hard from the fight but was far from spent. He wanted to tear these thugs apart, but Hatfield and his squire would pay with their lives if he did. It was obvious the attackers wanted to capture Rowan alive…probably for a ransom.

"Take our money and be gone." Rowan gripped his sword tightly. Every fiber in his body refused to let go of it.

The man holding the knife sneered at Rowan. "You're not listening."

He pressed the knife against Hatfield's throat until blood trickled down.

"Stop!" Rowan screamed.

The man just smiled and continued until Rowan could take it no more. He dropped his sword, and six brutes collapsed upon him in an instant. They bound his hands behind his back with thick ropes and looped another rope around his neck and down his back, tightly securing the end to the rope binding his hands. This made it difficult for him to move his arms much more than to allow a little slack in the rope around his neck.

When the ropes were secure, one of the men behind Rowan kicked his legs just behind his knees, forcing him into a kneeling position before their leader. The man played with the moneybag that had been retrieved from Rowan's horse.

"You have our money," Rowan said. "Now let us go."

The marauder to Rowan's left kicked him in the stomach so hard that he fell to the ground. The pain was so intense he thought he might be sick. He opened his eyes just in time to see another riveted leather boot smash into the right side of his face. A tooth in his lower jaw broke loose, and blood filled his mouth.

Rowan spit the tooth and blood on the ground, hoping the beating would stop. Two more kicks to his abdomen left him breathless.

"You are in no position to make demands!" the voice of his captor exclaimed.

Two men grabbed him by his arms and lifted him again to a kneeling

position. Rowan was dizzy with pain, teetering on the brink of uncon-
sciousness. The leader grabbed his chin and lifted it so he could look
into Rowan's eyes.

"Camerian hero—ha!" the man spit on Rowan's face, then motioned
to his companions. "Bring him. Kill the others."

"No!" Rowan screamed.

Hatfield and the squire struggled briefly, but two swords pierced
them each from behind. The look of absolute horror on their faces made
Rowan close his eyes and turn away, but the images remained etched in
his mind.

Rowan was placed on a horse and taken deeper into the forest. The
marauders stopped once they were well clear of the road and placed a
black bag over his head, then journeyed onward. For two days the
marauders traveled without giving Rowan any food or water. He thought
he would die of thirst. At last they stopped, pulled him off the horse and
onto the ground, and dragged him deep into a cavern that echoed with
each curse and footstep the marauders made. He was left facedown in
the dirt with the bag still over his head.

"Water…please," Rowan begged. His plea was rewarded with a
powerful kick to his unprotected ribs. He knew his ribs were bruised, if
not cracked, and the pain made his stomach churn. Footsteps echoed in
the cavern and faded away.

He wasn't sure how long he was unconscious, but he was glad for
the oblivion. Then he was jerked awake as hands brusquely grabbed his
arms and yanked him to a sitting position. The bag was removed, and
he blinked against the brilliant torchlight that burned his eyes. Two of
the men moved aside to allow their leader access to Rowan.

"The mighty Sir Rowan—a champion of Cameria." A black-haired
scoundrel with a full, scruffy beard paraded in front of Rowan, flaunt-
ing the victory cloak that now hung about his shoulders. "What do you
think? Does it look as good on me as it did on you?"

Anger burned in Rowan's bosom. How dare this lowly villain pre-
tend he could wear such a prize? The man stopped directly in front of
Rowan and looked down his nose at him, pretending to be a gallant

tournament knight. Then he whipped off the cloak, threw it down in front of Rowan, lifted his boot, and trampled it into the dirt.

"You think you are something special, but you are just Camerian scum."

The man knelt down close to his captive's face and smiled. Rowan raised his chin in defiance, and the man's smile contorted into a snarl.

"You arrogant Camerian," the man planted a fist into Rowan's face, reopening wounds from his previous beatings. Rowan's head jerked to the side; then he slowly turned back to face the man.

"I will collect a ransom for your life that will give Lord Malizimar and our allies enough money to continue our great work. Would you like to know what that great work is?"

Rowan just stared at the vengeful, weathered face. "It is the conquest of Cameria, the great evil eagle that is feeding Chessington and its pathetic pigs. You play in tournaments while my people die in starvation. Now you will live what our children live!"

The man made a fist and brought it close to Rowan's face. "Your life means nothing to me," he spat. "I would love to kill you along with every other Camerian, for you all disgust me!" The man reached down, lifted the cloak from the dirt, and rubbed it across Rowan's face.

"Your blood on your cloak will prove you are my prisoner. Your money will be mine, just as your life is mine!"

The man stood straight and walked to what looked like the entrance of the cave, though Rowan could see no light beyond it.

"Chain him up," the man said to his men. "When you're done, give him some water. He must at least be alive when they bring the money."

They replaced Rowan's ropes with chains, binding his wrists and ankles together, and secured him with another short chain to an iron stake in the ground. One of them poured fetid water from a dirty canteen into his mouth, nearly choking him in the process.

When they left with the torch, darkness swallowed him whole.

PRISON WITH NO END

Rowan had heard of Lord Malizimar and a region of people far to the southwest, near Chessington, but he had never given much thought to such faraway affairs. Why should a pauper-turned-champion care about such issues between people who were in constant strife?

He knew that the United Cities of Cameria supported Chessington, mostly because of the influence of the Knights of the Prince. Early on, it had seemed that nearly all of Cameria followed the Prince. In fact, being Camerian had been nearly synonymous with being a Follower. That had slowly changed, however, and support for Chessington from the masses had gradually diminished. In spite of this, the leadership of Cameria had continued to support Chessington and the King's people, and this had angered Lord Malizimar and his subjects. Now Rowan had somehow become entangled in the web of conflict on the far side of the kingdom, when the only thing he was guilty of was being successful and Camerian.

How long would it take for them to collect the ransom? As ruthless as these marauders seemed to be, Rowan doubted he would be set free even then. He figured his best chance was to escape on his own.

The fetters were too strong for him to break, but the stake was another matter. Rowan was strong—stronger perhaps than the marauders realized. If he could pull the stake from the ground…

He positioned himself directly over it, wrapped his hands around the short length of chain, took a deep breath, and pulled up with all of his might. His ribs burned with pain and he wanted to yell, but he dared not alarm his captors. He could feel his muscles strain as never before.

Just as he was about to give up, something moved ever so slightly. He relaxed and felt for the stake. It hadn't budged. But then he felt the link that attached his chain to the stake and realized it had opened just a sliver. It wasn't much, but it gave him the encouragement to try again.

He shook off the strain of the last attempt and gathered himself for another. After filling his lungs with the cave's dank air, he pulled up with every fiber of strength he had and felt the link give again, this time farther. He tried to pull his chain through the open link, but the opening was not yet wide enough. After one more mighty try, the chain slipped through the link, and he was free from the stake.

It was a moment of glorious hope. The short chain section between his ankles allowed him to take small steps. If he could escape out of the cave undetected, he might have a chance.

Rowan felt his way along the cave wall until he came to the alcove leading to another larger cavern. Then he hesitated as he realized that without a torch, he could easily walk right over a fifty-foot ledge to his death. The realization was nearly enough to cause him to turn back and wait for the guards to return, but then he realized that in chains his odds of overcoming two guards at once were slim at best.

He took a deep breath and maneuvered forward but stopped when he saw something quite remarkable. High above and before him were hundreds of soft blue glowing lights on what must be the ceiling of a large outer chamber. The glow wasn't strong enough to let him see anything directly in front of him, but it gave him a good idea where the cavern walls were and which direction to move.

Quietly and carefully, Rowan moved toward what seemed to be the far end of the cavern. After a few minutes he was directly beneath the glowing lights. What could make such a pleasant effect in such a forsaken place?

Just as he was about to continue, two of the blue lights above him began to move in tandem, obviously connected together. As they did, their glow brightened. Judging by the way the lights circled out into the dark and then returned, Rowan thought perhaps they belonged to some kind of unusual firefly. He watched in wonder as the dual light came closer, growing brighter with each passing moment. It passed directly over him, and he heard the flutter of soft wings.

Now six or so other pairs of lights began to move in circling flights above him. Mesmerized, he watched the cavern fill with hundreds of beautiful, glowing pairs of orbs.

Swish-thunk. Something large fluttered past him from behind and pricked the back of his neck.

"Ouch!" Rowan cried softly as the creature flew up and away from him. He caught a brief glimpse of a mothlike creature the size of a crow with dangling antennae that hung down from the back of its body. At the end of each antenna was a glowing, bulbous sac.

Rowan reached up to feel the back of his neck and felt warm fluid

oozing from a small puncture. He brought his hand to the front of his face and saw a glowing blue liquid mixed with blood on his fingers.

"What in the—" he exclaimed just as another set of wings fluttered near his left shoulder.

Swish-thunk.

"Ouch!" he exclaimed again. This time his left shoulder had been punctured. Rowan ducked down and began to bat at the flying orbs. Hundreds were diving down, and by their light he could just barely see the floor of the cave. He began to make his way through the tapered columns of rock, but something felt wrong, as if his chained feet had become stuck in mud.

The moths continued to dive. *Swish-thunk.* Another one hit his arm, and he swiped at it. Rowan tried to move away, but his legs wouldn't obey him. He felt himself falling and reached for a rock column to steady himself, but his arm would not lift up. He fell against the column and rolled to the ground on his back. His entire body was quickly becoming paralyzed.

"Help!" he called out, but it was a weak cry at best.

The moths swarmed above him, and he thought they might land on him and devour him in some horrid way. Instead, they hovered and then, one by one, alighted on the columns of stone nearby. Their wings flapped slowly and the orbs glowed even brighter, immersing him in a shower of beautiful blue light.

It took monumental effort to turn his head, and when he managed it, his gaze fell upon something horrific. The wall of the cavern was crawling with hundreds of foot-long caterpillars—all moving downward toward him. The caterpillars moved much like centipedes, with hundreds of legs moving in fluidic harmony to propel the creatures toward the blue light…and their meal.

Rowan tried to yell again, but he could not make his mouth form the sound. He tried to roll away from the wall, but his body wouldn't move. Some of the caterpillars were now at the base of the cavern wall and crawling toward him on the ground. Fear overwhelmed him as he watched his horrific fate unfold.

"Though you can't move or scream, you will feel every bite these nasty little creatures take."

Rowan heard a voice mock him from the side of the cavern opposite the approaching caterpillars. "It won't take long, though." The man laughed, and another voice joined in. "Only an hour or two."

The caterpillars were now just three paces away.

The bright yellow light of a lantern suddenly mixed with the blue. Most of the moths fluttered and took flight.

"The only thing that will stop the moths is bright light," Rowan heard the bearded marauder say. "But there is nothing that can stop the flesh-eating caterpillars."

Rowan felt a rough hand grab his chin and turn his head away from his approaching doom. The bearded man's face appeared, smiling sadistically. Rowan pleaded with his eyes for help.

"Promise not to try and escape again?" the marauder teased. "Because if you do"—the man flipped Rowan's head back toward the caterpillars, now only two paces away—"I will not stop them again."

The caterpillars were close enough for Rowan to see powerful mandibles opening and closing in anticipation of their feast. They were almost upon him, and Rowan was in near panic.

"Drag him back to the cave," the bearded man ordered as he stood up.

Rowan waited, but nothing happened until the first caterpillar reached his leg. Then he felt his shoulders lift up and his body began to move, but not before the creature's powerful jaws chomped into his leg. Pain pierced through him, and he wanted to scream but couldn't.

Much to his relief, the bearded man kicked the caterpillar away from Rowan, then yelled and held a lighted torch down at the ground toward the army of crawling creatures. The light seemed to halt them, at least for a minute. Rowan felt himself being dragged, and he watched as whoever was pulling him slowly outdistanced the caterpillars. The light of the lantern and the torches the men were carrying illumined the cavern enough for Rowan to see hundreds of cocoons hanging from the ceiling. Some were splitting open to reveal young moths spreading their new wings.

Rowan felt himself sag with relief when they finally made it back to the cave where he had been imprisoned. The bearded man pointed his sword at Rowan's throat. "You're lucky you're worth a lot of money to me," he said. "Don't be stupid again. I don't give second chances."

He sneered at Rowan and turned away. "Chain him up again. This time make it so he can't stand up."

Rowan lay in the dark, unable to move, for a long while after the marauders left. As the hours passed, he gradually regained control of his body, though he was tied so tightly he still could not move much. His mind raced, trying to fathom what had just happened to him.

He had been through a horrific experience, one he knew he would never forget, and he had no idea what would happen next. His only hope now was that Balenteen had escaped and would negotiate to pay his ransom.

Time crept by as Rowan lay there in utter darkness, with no way of knowing how long he was held prisoner. Occasionally he heard creatures scurrying across the floor, and he shuddered when one brushed up against his leg. Every so often he would hear voices in the distance or the flutter of bat wings. It was the occasional squealing of rats that shook Rowan the most, however, for he imagined that they often fell prey to the glowing moths and caterpillars. A captured rat would squeal frantically for a short time, then slowly the screams would fade away to silence.

The marauders came each day and loosened him from the short chain that bound him to the stake and allowed him to walk about the cave in fetters. They gave Rowan only enough food and water to keep him alive. His howling hunger faded gradually to a dull ache, but thirst was ever with him. His tongue and mouth were so dry that they stuck to each other. He dreaded the visits from the bearded man, who never failed to insult and beat him. Each beating was worse than the previous one, for the man seemed to grow more and more frustrated.

Rowan grew weaker and weaker, withering away in the darkness until his arms and legs weren't much thicker than bone. By the growth of his beard, he guessed that many weeks had passed, and he began to lose hope. Where was Balenteen?

To keep himself from going insane, Rowan relived the glory days of his tournaments over and over in his mind. But as the weeks turned to months, his tournament memories seemed so far in the past that he began to wonder if he'd even lived them at all.

Then, finally, the bearded leader of the marauders came to kill him.

SEVEN

JOURNEY
OF DREAMS

 For nearly a year I have waited for the promise of your ransom, and for all of my trouble with you I have gained nothing!" The bearded man was in a fury. Rowan just lay in a fetal position, hoping the end would be swift.

"Your own people don't think enough of you to even pay for the food I've fed you—you pathetic, worthless Camerian!" The enraged man drew his sword to plunge it into Rowan's heart. Rowan opened his arms to welcome the blade.

The man hesitated. "Why don't you cower?"

"Kill me," Rowan begged with a weak voice.

The man slowly lowered his sword and began to smile. He stepped backward away from Rowan.

"Kill me!" Rowan begged again.

"I am." The man gave a short laugh, then turned and left, the light of his torch flickering and fading away.

Rowan realized the marauders would never be back. His cruel execution from thirst and starvation would be their last horrific act. In his condition, it would not take long—perhaps a day or two.

As he lay there in the dark, Rowan wondered about the purpose of his life and realized that all his glorious trophies and medals, the applause of thousands, and the admiration of squires and maidens alike meant nothing to him. Only then did he realize that he truly had taken only one significant action in his life, and that was to become a Follower of the Prince. It was that day that he joined something larger than himself. *Why did it take so long and so much pain for me to finally understand this?* he wondered.

"What a fool I've been," he whispered in the darkness. "Forgive me, my Prince. If I could live another life, I would live it wholly committed to You. Forgive me."

Rowan wept softly at first and then uncontrollably—dry, tearless sobs that hurt his chest. His wails echoed off the walls of his small chamber and into the cavern beyond. Eventually, his cries softened into sighs of relinquishment. Curling up quietly on the hard dirt floor, Rowan finally released himself to the death that awaited him. His mind wallowed in the fringes between life and death, hallucinating in freedom from the chains and the darkness of the cave that would be his grave.

The cave began to glow, and the rocky walls melted into the fluid movements of silky curtains. He was traveling, for he could feel the bed he was on jostle as he journeyed down a road. The water he tasted was sweet, and he breathed deeply of the fresh spring air. He didn't want to wake up, but keeping the dream going took too much effort. Soon the images of delight faded once again into the dark walls of his cave.

When he dreamed again, he could feel the rhythmic mass of the sea swaying him on a grand ship. The mist of the open water felt so real on his face. He had never been to sea and wondered if his dream was anything like the real thing. This time the beauty of his dreamscape faded as a dark figure came and stood over him. The face was blurred, but Rowan was certain the bearded marauder had come once more to kill his unransomed captive. This time, however, he heard cries and screams in the distance that shook his soul. He struggled weakly, but powerful arms held him down, and he waited for the knife that would plunge into his heart.

"—near the Isle of Sedah. It is not far—"

The fragment of speech swirled in his mind, and Rowan could

make no sense of it until he remembered something from his training. The Isle of Sedah was the horrific place of captivity to which the Dark Knight, Lucius, had brought many prisoners. Had Rowan somehow been given over to Lucius to be tortured even more? He tried to awake from this nightmare, and finally the images and sounds faded away to blackness.

Now Rowan heard drums pounding in his head, but each beat transformed into sounds that he could understand. Then he realized it was not a drum he was hearing, but the sound of a deep voice speaking over him.

"What are your orders, my Lord?" the voice asked.

"Leave him here with me," another replied.

Rowan blinked his eyes open, and the sun spilled its glorious light into them. The sunrays warmed his face, and he wondered how long this dream would last. He took a deep breath. It felt so real.

He turned his head and saw the most beautiful sight he had ever seen—a magnificent city on a hill, glimmering in the brilliant sunlight. The wall that surrounded the city stretched left and right forever. Through a massive, shining gate that faced him, he caught glimpses of unimaginable splendor, yet somehow the whole place seemed warm and welcoming, not the least intimidating.

Tears welled up in his eyes, but he didn't know why—perhaps because he knew this would be his last dream. He was thankful to end his life with this instead of the previous nightmare.

"Hello, Rowan," a gentle voice spoke.

Rowan turned his head to the other side, away from the city, and saw a man sitting on the green grass beside him. The man's arm lay across his raised knee, and his face seemed to reflect the sunlight just as the city's golden gate did.

Rowan didn't respond. He just marveled at the man, who leaned in closer. "How are you feeling?"

Rowan turned his head in the other direction, fully expecting the city to be gone, but it was still there. He looked back at the man. "Am I dead?" he finally asked.

The man smiled. "Come, sit up…if you are able."

He reached an arm behind Rowan's shoulders and slowly lifted him. Rowan's head swam, and he put out a hand to his head to steady himself. "That's strange," he said. "I didn't think one could pass out in a dream."

"You're not dreaming, Rowan," the man said. "You are at the gates of the King's city."

Rowan shook his head, trying to understand what was happening. He looked into the eyes of the man.

"I've heard your voice before," he said warily. "You were the one I fought…in the arena…and on the road!"

"Yes, you had lost your way." The man's gentle voice grew stronger as Rowan gathered his strength. "You should have turned back."

"You were trying to…to help me?"

The man nodded, and his warm eyes seemed to penetrate into the very depths of Rowan's soul. Rowan tilted his head as it dawned on him who the stranger might be. Even if this were a dream, he could only respond one way. He lowered his head, and tears fell from his face.

"I'm sorry, my Prince. Please forgive me."

The Prince placed a hand across the back of Rowan's neck, and He leaned toward him until His forehead touched Rowan's. "I forgive you," He whispered.

"I wasted my life on frivolous applause and pieces of metal, and now it is over." Rowan's heart ached for the life he hadn't lived.

The Prince squeezed his neck, then released him. He reached for a water flask and gave it to Rowan.

"Be at peace, Rowan. Drink."

Rowan placed the flask to his lips and drank deeply of the sweet water. The Prince lowered him back, and Rowan realized he was lying on a cot.

"Your life is not over, for you are a mighty knight of the King. Time is short, and I have a mission that awaits you in Arrethtrae."

Rowan felt confusion wash over him, and the world melted away once more. His last conscious thought was a sad one: he hated to leave this sweet final dream. ▨

EIGHT

A SONG IN THE DARK

Rowan opened his eyes, but the blackness of the cave suffocated him once more. Something crawled across his face, and he didn't even swipe it away. The heavy irons still hung on his ankles and wrists.

Death teased him, though in fact he felt more alive now than he had in a long time. Why had he dreamed such a vivid dream about the Prince? His dreamed emotions of regret and renewal seemed quite hollow and meaningless now.

He closed his eyes and waited. How many more days of this torture would he have to endure? He tried to return to the freedom of his dreams, but they eluded him.

He lay in silence for a very long while until he thought perhaps he was hallucinating again. The faint, lilting sounds of an angelic singing voice sifted through the darkness and lit upon his ears. Rowan sat up, and the chains jingled, momentarily blocking out the lovely voice. He listened again, hoping he had not silenced the lilting voice, whether dream or not.

Then he heard it again. Could it be real?

"Help!" he croaked, his voice hoarse with disuse. Was it loud enough to carry out of his cave past the larger cavern and out into the open air?

"Help!" he tried again, trying for more volume.

The singing stopped, so he cried once more, as loudly as he could. "Help!"

"Hello?" a faint but lovely voice beckoned from the darkness. "Is someone there?"

"Yes. Please help me!" Rowan rasped. Hope welled up painfully in his heart. "Please help!"

"Are you trapped?" she called.

"Yes. Please…"

"I'm coming," she called back.

He had been tricked before by his own hallucinations and wondered if this was another cruel joke of death.

"Keep talking," the voice called. "Where are you?"

"I'm in a cave at the back of the—stop!" Rowan's stomach rose up to his throat as he realized the danger. Too late. He heard the woman scream.

"What has happened?" he called out, but he knew the answer. "Get out of the cave while you can still move!"

Over the next few moments, Rowan pulled against his chains in anguish as he tried to interpret the muffled sounds from the outer cavern.

"Leave the cave!" he called back in desperation.

The woman cried out something, but it was unintelligible, and Rowan closed his eyes in despair. He could not bear to think of the horrid death the woman was about to endure.

"My Prince," he whispered, "where are You?"

Hours passed as he lay there, trying not to think of what was happening in the cavern outside. Then a faint glow of yellow light spilled into his cave. "Are you still there?" the woman's voice called out.

Rowan couldn't believe his ears.

"Yes…yes. I'm here. In this cave."

Rowan's cave soon filled with light, and he blinked as he set his eyes upon the slender form of a young woman carrying a lantern and a shovel. He struggled to gain his feet but could barely manage to sit up.

"You…you survived!" he said.

"Obviously," the woman said.

"Are you real?" His voice quavered. "Or am I dreaming again?"

Shadows danced off the woman's face as she scrutinized him.

"I am real," she said carefully, "and you are not dreaming."

"They said nothing could stop the caterpillars. How did you…?"

"I fell onto the white path that led here. They wouldn't come onto the path. I think it is covered in salt. Perhaps that's what kept them away."

The woman took a deep breath as if to shake the jitters from her. "It was quite ghastly, lying there for hours, hoping those nasty things wouldn't eat me." She made a disgusted face, then narrowed her eyes. "You said you were trapped, not chained," she said. "Why are you here?"

"Marauders killed my men and stole everything. They are…were holding me for ransom."

The woman raised a skeptical eyebrow.

"I swear it is true," Rowan said in desperation.

After a moment of silent contemplation, she seemed to grow anxious. She looked behind her as if she might leave. Rowan held out his hand.

"Please…please don't leave me," he pleaded. "They left me to die days ago—at least I think it was days. Please help me."

The woman settled a bit, looked at Rowan once more, and took a deep breath as if to accept the duty.

"My name's Mariah."

"I am Rowan…of Laos."

His name clearly meant nothing to her. She set the lantern down and cautiously approached Rowan, the shovel before her. When she saw his emaciated state, she relaxed her guard. Rowan stared at her as if she might disappear at any moment. When she hesitated, he broke his gaze and lifted the chains.

"They are strong—too strong to break, I fear."

"Perhaps we can dig the stake out," she offered.

"I have tried to do that with my hands, but the ground was too hard. It is worth a try with the shovel."

Mariah set to the task. Rowan could offer no help. It wasn't long before it became obvious that her digging was not working.

Mariah swiped beads of sweat from her brow. "It's impossible," she said. She sat down, deep in thought. "At the entrance to the cavern there were things strewn about. Perhaps the keys to your locks are there."

She set the shovel against the wall and lifted the lantern. Rowan felt sick at the thought of being left in the dark again. She looked at him and seemed to read his thoughts.

"I promise I will come back."

"Thank you, Mariah," he said quietly.

Mariah gave a quick grin and nodded, then disappeared into the outer cavern. Rowan waited anxiously until she appeared again.

"Were there keys?" he asked.

"No, but I found this." She held up a long stake, similar to the one Rowan was chained to.

"How will that help us?"

Mariah inserted the tip of the free stake into the chain link closest to the ground and began to twist the link until it was bound upon itself. Then she used the stake as a lever, putting all of her weight on the other end. After two tries, the link snapped, and Rowan was free. He stayed sitting on the ground for a moment, wondering if he remembered how to stand erect. He slowly stood up, but his knees buckled. Mariah reached out to steady him.

"Are you all right?" she asked.

Rowan closed his eyes and nodded. "But I'm not sure that I can walk."

"Here, I'll help you." She positioned herself under his arm so that he could lean against her. Then, very slowly, they moved along the white salt path that led to the front of the cavern. Hundreds of moths circled above but did not come close enough to threaten them.

They finally reached the cavern entrance. Rowan fell to his knees and turned his face upward to the blue sky. He blinked, nearly blinded by the late afternoon sun, but still rejoicing in his freedom. Mariah left him there and retrieved her horse. She rummaged in the saddlebags and handed him her water bottle and part of a biscuit.

He started to guzzle the water, but Mariah pulled it away from him.

"You must go slowly, or you will be sick." She seemed fairly appalled at the sight of him now that she could fully see his feeble, filthy state.

Rowan nodded and took small nibbles of the biscuit, followed by shallow drinks of water.

"You ride Sierra," Mariah said. "Once we get to my farm, we'll get the rest of your chains off."

Mounting the horse was problematic because of Rowan's physical state and his leg chains, but with Mariah's help he finally managed to perch sidesaddle and lean heavily on the animal's neck. Exhaustion was quickly overtaking him, and he wondered if he would even be able to ride very far.

With frequent stops and much patience on Mariah's part, they finally made it to her farmhouse. Rowan nearly fell from the horse, not caring if he even made it indoors, but Mariah refused to give up. She all but carried him inside and to a bed. The glorious softness of the mattress beneath him pulled him to slumber. He was vaguely aware that Mariah was occupied with various tasks nearby, but he didn't care. He just hoped that the bed wouldn't fade to rock and dirt again.

NINE

HOMEWARD BOUND

 When Rowan awoke, at first he didn't dare open his eyes.

Please let this be real, he pleaded within himself.

Then the delightful sound of Mariah's voice filled the air with song and his heart with gladness. He finally opened his eyes to see the beautiful smile of his rescuer.

"Good morning," Mariah said.

Rowan filled his lungs with delicious air.

"I have a surprise for you." She lifted his hand into the air.

The shackles were gone. He looked at his feet, and they were unfettered too.

"I don't know how I can thank you." Rowan rubbed his abraded wrists and looked up at her. To him, at that moment, she was the most beautiful woman he had ever seen. Blue eyes peered at him from behind loose tousles of dark brown hair. She was tall, slender but strong, and though the features of her face were feminine, they were also quite distinctive, with high, slanted cheekbones and a generous mouth that revealed dimples when she smiled.

"Why don't you sit up if you can?" she said. "I have some breakfast for you, but you must remember to eat slowly."

Mariah helped him sit up and propped a pillow behind him. Then she brought a tray with a glass of diluted juice and a small bowl of warm corn mush with stewed fruit. To Rowan it looked like a meal fit for a king. He looked back up at Mariah. She smiled and tilted her head, then sat down in a chair next to him.

"Do you have a family here with you?" he asked, peering down the hallway behind her.

Mariah hesitated. "Since you're certainly not much of a threat right now, I guess I can tell you I am alone here."

"I'm sorry to be such a burden to you," Rowan said. "I'll leave straightaway."

Mariah raised an eyebrow. "You wouldn't make it ten feet past the front door in your condition. You can stay in this spare room until you're strong enough to move about. After that, I've an outbuilding that would suit well until you can travel."

Rowan nodded. "I'm very grateful for your kindness."

"When you're ready, there is water for washing…and some clothes in the armoire." Mariah nodded with her head to the corner of the room.

Rowan glanced at the armoire and back at Mariah with a puzzled look on his face. She dropped her gaze to her hands. "My husband died late last summer."

"I…I'm sorry," Rowan said.

Mariah nodded and blinked back tears, then forced a smile. "I've considered leaving the farm and joining my family, but that seems like giving up on Palson. He worked hard to build this farm, and we've only been here two seasons. I just can't leave—not yet anyway. I've decided to try it one season, and then…I'll know."

"You're a courageous woman, Mariah."

She blinked again, took a deep breath, and looked at Rowan. Her eyes narrowed. "So what's your story? Where are you from?"

Rowan carefully lifted the glass of juice and drank. He could feel the cool, soothing liquid run down his insides and settle into his stomach. It was a strange sensation.

"As a child, I was an orphan, living on the streets of Laos. But then I met a man who taught me about the Prince."

Mariah's eyes opened wide. She leaned forward and put her hand on his arm. "The King reigns…," she began.

"And His Son," Rowan finished.

"So you're a Follower too?" she asked

Rowan dropped his gaze. "Yes…but not a very good one." He looked back into her eyes and saw no condemnation.

"Sir Aldwyn took me under his tutelage and taught me the ways of the Prince and of the sword." Rowan paused to take a bite of his corn mush. "I learned them well, especially the sword. After four-and-a-half years of training, I began to participate in the tournaments."

At that, Mariah looked confused. "Why?" she asked.

Rowan wasn't sure how to answer. She had obviously never heard of him, and he found himself grateful for that. "Because I was a foolish young knight seeking fame and fortune." He grimaced and turned away for a moment.

"So," Mariah asked teasingly, "did you find it?"

He looked back into her eyes.

"Yes."

Mariah's smile faded as she realized that he was not kidding.

"I know it is hard to believe, considering how I look now." Rowan lifted a wasted arm and shook his head. "But before my capture, I was quite strong. I fought in many tournaments and eventually became the champion of Laos. I was on my way to fight in the Camerian Games at Kroywen when I was taken by the marauders."

Mariah slowly straightened in her chair. Rowan wondered if she believed him. His story sounded far-fetched even to him. Nothing was said for a while as Rowan took another drink of juice and finished a few spoonfuls of mush.

"I will be able to pay you for your trouble once I get back to Laos," Rowan said.

Mariah reached for the empty tray across Rowan's lap. "Palson said we shouldn't accept payment for kindness, especially from those who are in need." She stood and started toward the door. "You are welcome to stay as long as you like, provided you behave yourself."

It took Rowan a week before he felt he had regained enough strength to move about and relocate to the outbuilding. He still fatigued easily, but he could feel his strength steadily returning. Mariah's care was unfaltering, and Rowan became more and more grateful to her every day. Hearing her sing in the morning was perhaps his favorite experience of each day, for it was a reminder that he was indeed free from the torture of evil men.

The more he was with Mariah, in fact, the more he liked her. At first he attributed the attraction to the fact that she had saved his life and was caring for him, but then he began to suspect it was something more. None of the other maidens of Laos had ever affected him this way. Mariah was a true Follower of the Prince, and he admired how she lived her simple life with integrity and devotion. He also admired her beauty, and each day he found himself drawn to her more strongly.

She, on the other hand, seemed to be distancing herself from him as he grew stronger, and he couldn't understand why. She gave no indication that he was anything more than a guest in need. He told himself this was probably for the best, since his life in Laos was waiting for him.

When ten days had passed, Rowan decided to return home. He voiced his intentions the next morning at breakfast.

"You're still in no condition to travel," Mariah protested mildly. "I could barely get you from the cave to my farm, and that's a short distance compared to the journey to Laos. It's a full day's ride even for a healthy man."

He had learned earlier from Mariah that her farm was southwest of Laos, on the edge of the Altica Valley.

"I appreciate your concern, Mariah, but I have to go home and recover my estate."

He expected her to protest further, but she did not. She gazed at him thoughtfully and then nodded. "I understand and agree. But I can't afford to give you a horse, and you'll never make it on your own. I'll make arrangements with my neighbors to the north to care for the farm, then travel with you to Laos."

"I would be most grateful…again," he said with a smile, and she smiled back. He caught himself staring into her delightful blue eyes, then decided to focus on his breakfast.

"Rowan?" Her voice had become soft and serious.

"I went to a tournament once, years ago. It seemed rather… Well, I guess what I'm trying to ask is, what kind of a man were you before you were captured?"

Rowan looked up from his food, wishing she hadn't asked him such a penetrating question. There was still so much to sort out. He frowned.

"You don't have to answer that," Mariah said. "I'm sorry… It's none of my business, and you've been through much."

She lifted her plate and stood up from the table, but Rowan reached out and grabbed her arm. "I want to answer it," he said.

She slowly sat back down. He pulled back his arm and took a deep breath.

"I was a man who loved the applause of the crowds, the wealth and trophies of my winnings, and the attention of the maidens. At first, when I became a Knight of the Prince, my heart was right, but as I realized that my gift with the sword and the strength of my body was something unique, I began to…'lose my way,' as a friend once said."

Rowan hesitated as he thought of Sir Aldwyn. He wondered what his mentor would think of him now.

"I convinced myself that because I had been a street urchin, I deserved the fame and wealth of a tournament champion. And I told myself I could pursue it without compromising as a Knight of the Prince." He shook his head and shot a crooked a smile at her. "Perhaps there are men out there who can do it, but I could not. I didn't realize how lost I was until long after I had been chained in that cave."

Rowan shrugged sheepishly.

She didn't smile. "Are you still that man?" she asked.

Rowan met her eyes; then his gaze fell to the table. It was a fair question, one he hadn't dared ask himself. His dream of his time with the Prince still echoed in his mind, but how much could a dream change a man?

"I don't know," he finally answered her. "That cave…those chains… my dreams… I don't want to be that former man, but I guess I have nothing to prove I'm any different. Not yet anyway."

She said nothing, merely nodded and picked up her plate again. Numbly he watched her go. It was the first time in many years that he had felt so…lacking. He had nothing to offer her that she would care to receive. A woman of her caliber would have no interest in wealth. She would rather have a pauper with a pure and humble heart—one fully committed to the Prince.

If the cost of such a heart were all of my fame and wealth, he wondered, *would I make the trade?*

The next day, Rowan and Mariah packed two of her horses and set off for Laos. Mariah was still concerned about his ability to travel, and the journey did prove much more difficult for Rowan than he expected, but he pushed himself so they could make Laos by sundown. They arrived on the ridge of a hill overlooking the city just as daylight faded and lights began to appear in houses.

An entire mix of emotions flooded through Rowan as he prepared to return home, but anticipation dominated them all and renewed his strength a bit. He wondered if Balenteen had made it back to town and, if so, how well he had preserved his estate. What of the tournaments? What would be expected of him? Could or would he return to tournament life? Did he even want to?

Laos was a sprawling city with ten thousand lanterns already burning in defiance of the fading light of the day. Rowan felt like he might collapse at any moment, but the sight of the city spurred him on. Mariah look concerned but said nothing.

"Eastgate is my estate," he told her. "It's on the eastern edge of the city, facing the mountains."

They skirted the city along the southeast. As they neared Rowan's property, they passed many homes, and Mariah gawked in wonder at the obvious wealth of the area.

"We're nearly there," Rowan assured her. "We can—"

"Halt!" A mounted guard in an unfamiliar uniform was blocking their way. Rowan had seen others like him on their trek around the city, but he hadn't thought much of it until now.

The man approached them with an air of authority. "State the nature of your business."

Rowan glanced over at Mariah, who shrugged. "Why?" he asked.

The guard's countenance grew stern. "State the nature of your business *now*!"

Rowan hesitated, perturbed at the guard's absurd request. "I am Sir Rowan," he finally said, "and I am traveling to my estate."

The guard looked skeptical. "Give me your citizen papers."

Rowan just looked at the man. "I haven't the foggiest idea what you are talking about," he replied.

At that the guard drew his sword and held it at ready. "Prefect Corsan has ordered all people of Laos to register as citizens," he said. "Without your papers you are not allowed to travel anywhere. You are in violation of that edict—and numerous others, I'm sure. You will come with me."

Rowan took a deep breath, his frustration vying with his fatigue. Something had obviously changed in his absence.

"I have been away for a very long time," he said. "I am tired and just want to go home. My estate, Eastgate, is just over there." Rowan pointed toward a large, opulent manor behind a gilded gate. "You can follow us if you'd like, and I'll prove it to you."

The guard hesitated, looked toward the estate, and sheathed his sword. "You'd better be telling the truth, or you'll be spending time in the prison."

Rowan suppressed a laugh. He spurred his horse past the guard and traveled on toward his gate. When Rowan dismounted, he had to clutch at the saddle to keep from falling to the ground. Mariah jumped off her horse to help him.

The guard followed them up to the door of the manor, and Rowan tried to open it, but it was locked. He knocked, and soon the door opened slightly. A servant's face appeared.

"I am Sir Rowan. This is my estate. Open the door and let me through."

"Wait here." The servant closed the door and disappeared. Rowan leaned against the brick portico.

"Are you all right, Rowan?" Mariah asked.

Rowan took a breath. He needed to lie down soon.

A moment later the door opened again. "What is the meaning of this?" a voice demanded.

There stood Balenteen in regal clothing. "Who are you people?" he demanded.

"Balenteen, it is I, Sir Rowan. Thank goodness you survived." Rowan stepped forward and tried to enter, but Balenteen stood in the way.

"Sentinel, remove these people from my property. I don't know who they are." Balenteen slammed the door before Rowan could respond.

He began pounding on the door, but the sentinel grabbed him and began to pull him away.

"Balenteen, you traitor!" Rowan shouted. "You thief! This is my estate!"

After a brief struggle, Rowan stumbled and fell to one knee. His face turned downward to the ground as he tried to hold himself up.

"You will come with me to the consulate," the sentinel said firmly.

Mariah put an arm about Rowan to keep him from completely collapsing. She looked up at the sentinel with pleading eyes. "Please, sir, you can see that he is very sick. Let me take care of him."

"Without papers or verification I have no choice. You may be an enemy of the city." The sentinel seemed unsure what to do. Rowan was clearly in no condition to travel.

The sentinel looked up and down the roadway, then mounted his horse. "Wait here until I return. Do not leave, or your fate will be much worse when I find you."

The sentinel galloped off to the west. Rowan leaned against Mariah, his only friend in all the kingdom.

TEN

THE WORK OF ONE

 We must leave, Rowan," Mariah pleaded. "The sentinel will be back any moment. I'll help you mount Sierra."

"I can't," Rowan murmured, slumping closer toward the ground. He seemed to have hit an emotional and physical brick wall.

Mariah leaned him against a lamppost and paced nearby, searching the roadway for sentinels. Rowan felt like his body was made of lead. All he wanted to do was lie down and close his eyes. Even breathing felt like an ordeal.

How could Balenteen have betrayed me? he fumed through the haze of his exhaustion. No wonder the ransom had never been paid. Balenteen must have been hoping the marauders would kill him. And Balenteen was fortunate, because if Rowan had any strength left in his body, the evening would have turned violent.

Rowan looked over at Mariah and felt sorry for her. She had not chosen this situation; Rowan had pulled her into it.

She came and knelt down beside him. "You spoke of a Sir Aldwyn once. We can go to his house." But Rowan had begun to fade.

"Rowan! You have to get up." Her voice was tight with worry. "The sentinels are coming!"

The idea of standing, let alone mounting a horse, seemed impossible. Rowan shook his head. "I can't. Take your horses and leave me, Mariah." He closed his eyes. "I'm sorry to have brought this on you. You go. Once they discover who I am, everything will be all right."

Mariah grabbed the collar of his tunic and came to within inches of his face. He opened his eyes to see a fiery resolve he had never expected.

"I don't think they're planning on letting you go, and I didn't risk my life in the moth cave to see you taken prisoner again." Mariah pulled on his tunic until he was on his knees. "What sort of a champion are you? Now get up!"

She wrapped his left arm around her shoulder and forced him to stand with her. Out of sheer determination, she pulled, pushed, taunted, and encouraged him until he was precariously perched upon his horse once more.

"Tell me where Sir Aldwyn lives," she said as she led their horses down the street in the opposite direction from the one the sentinel had traveled. She rode close to Rowan's side, trying to keep him upright.

"Go north"—Rowan could hardly form the words—"across the eastern bridge…"

Mariah led them as quickly as possible to the north, skirting much of the city. Twice she was forced to divert to avoid more sentinels. Finally, after what seemed like an agonizingly long ride, they arrived at Sir Aldwyn's modest home.

Mariah leaned Rowan against the doorpost, then quickly tied the two horses at the back of the home so as not to draw any undue attention. No matter what they found here, this would be the end of their travels tonight, for Rowan was spent.

Mariah returned and knocked on the door. At first it seemed that no one was home, but after a second attempt, the door opened a crack.

"What do you want?" a quavering voice asked from the shadow of the doorway.

"We're looking for Sir Aldwyn," Mariah said.

"No one here by that name." The old woman began to close the door.

Did the entire kingdom change while I was away? Rowan wondered.

"I am Sir Rowan, a former squire of Sir Aldwyn." His words were weak and slurred, but they stopped the door from completely closing. After a moment of motionless silence, the old woman spoke softly.

"The work of One saves many," she said tentatively.

It was an odd statement, and Rowan's head swam in confusion and frustration. Was this some sort of pass code?

"We are the many," Mariah quietly replied.

The door opened. "Come in quickly," the old woman said. Her countenance was serious but not unkind. The creases around her eyes and lips told of tense and anxious days.

Mariah helped Rowan stumble through the door.

"I'm Zetta," the old woman said, quickly closing the door behind them.

"Thank you, Madam Zetta," Mariah said. "He needs to lie down."

"This way." The woman picked up a lantern and led them down a hallway into a bedchamber. Rowan fell upon the bed and didn't move.

"There's another chamber just down the hall for you, young lady," he heard the elderly woman say.

"Thank you, madam," Mariah replied. "I'm going to make sure he's all right before I…"

The words faded away as Rowan drifted to something much deeper than mere sleep.

When Rowan awoke, his body felt pinned to the bed, and he had to look to see if his shackles had reappeared on his ankles and wrists. With each passing moment, however, he started to feel better. He brought himself to a sitting position just as someone knocked on the door.

"Come in," he called.

"Well, that's an improvement," Mariah said as she entered the room. "Are you able to eat something? Zetta has made a delicious breakfast."

Rowan managed a smile. "That would be wonderful."

"Shall I bring it to you, or can you make it to the table?"

"I think I can get to the table…with a little help," he said.

She helped him to his feet, but before they took their first step together, Rowan hesitated. "Mariah, I've never needed help from anyone, and I've never had anyone take care of me before."

Mariah looked up at him as if she were waiting for the punch line, but Rowan just gazed gently into her eyes. "Thank you," he said and felt her arm soften around his waist as they began their careful walk down the hallway and into the kitchen.

At the breakfast table, Rowan felt some of his strength returning. "Madam Zetta, thank you for allowing us into your home."

"You are welcome, but it is not my home," Zetta replied. "It is Sir Aldwyn's."

"I thought you said—"

"I said he is not here…but the home is still his. He's asked me to stay behind and help people like you…Resolutes."

"So, it's true after all." Mariah stared at Zetta.

Rowan looked at Mariah, perplexed. "What's true?"

"My father heard rumors that Kroywen had a new prefect who had dissolved many of the people's freedoms," she said. "I had no idea Laos had fallen to the same fate," Mariah said.

"Yes," Zetta replied. "Only just recently, though. Sir Aldwyn saw it coming and began preparing. Resolutes began to gather. We must be very careful."

Rowan stared at Mariah, amazed by something even deeper in her character than he expected. "You knew the pass code," he said.

Mariah nodded. "From my father. My mother died years ago. Six months ago, when my father and my brother heard what was happening at Kroywen, they went to join the Resolutes—to try to stop the takeover of Cameria." Mariah stared down at the table. "My father loves this land and the freedom it stands for. He served in the Camerian army before he was a farmer. Nothing could keep him from joining the Resolutes."

"He left you alone?" Rowan asked bewildered.

"No. Palson and I were to farm the land until my father and brother returned, but…" Mariah hesitated. "Just two months after my father and brother left, Palson was bitten by a mountain asp. I…I couldn't save him."

Zetta reached over and took Mariah's hands in hers. "I'm so sorry, child."

Mariah accepted the consolation gratefully. "I have to keep the farm going until they return." Mariah looked over at Rowan. "When you wanted to go to Laos to recover your estate, I thought it would be an opportunity to see for myself what was really happening." Mariah shook her head. "It's much worse than I suspected."

Rowan took a deep breath and sat back in his chair, trying to put everything together in his head. "Who is doing this to Cameria?" he asked.

"As near as we can tell, much of the influence is coming from Lord Malizimar's region near Daydelon," Zetta said.

Lord Malizimar. The name hit Rowan like a brick.

"The marauders who captured me claimed they were supporting Lord Malizimar and his cause." He put his hand to his head as he tried to piece it all together. "But why?"

"Chessington," Mariah and Zetta both said at the same time.

"Cameria supports Chessington and the King's people there. Lord Malizimar hates Chessington and wants to conquer it. Cameria stands in his way."

"I find it difficult to believe that you were a squire under Sir Aldwyn for so many years and he didn't tell you these things," Zetta said with a tone that was nearly a reprimand.

Rowan felt his cheeks flush slightly. "He tried, but I didn't hear much of it. I was too concerned with learning the sword and how to fight in tournaments." Rowan rubbed the back of his neck. "Where is Sir Aldwyn now?"

"Sir Aldwyn's gone to join the Resolutes, too," Zetta added. "And he's left me here to help others who will join the cause. Prefect Corsan and his sentinels wouldn't suspect an old woman like me of doing them any harm or the Resolutes any good, but I have my part and I will play it well!" Zetta's face gleamed with the confidence and determination of a gallant knight.

Rowan felt small in every way. He had been self-consumed before his capture, and afterward he had been caught up with regaining what he considered rightfully his—while many around him were sacrificing everything to save the freedom of people they didn't even know. He lowered his gaze to the table and fell silent.

"Are you feeling all right?" Mariah asked.

Rowan looked up at her. "Not really." He gave her a weak smile. "I think I need to lie down again."

Mariah rose up to help him. He motioned her away and tried to make it on his own, but he faltered. Mariah reached for him, and he sighed. He was tired of being weak.

"Rowan," Zetta called as he and Mariah turned toward the hallway. "I don't think Sir Aldwyn expected you to come here. He was told that you were dead."

"That would be the lying work of Balenteen, my ex-tournament agent."

"I should think that Sir Aldwyn would be delighted to see you again someday," Zetta said with a kind smile.

Rowan remembered their last parting and wasn't so sure. He just nodded, then turned and shuffled toward his bedchamber, with Mariah's support. She helped him settle to his bed, checking his forehead for signs of a fever. Rowan looked up at her, feeling rather ashamed for who he was and how he'd lived.

"Palson was a good man, wasn't he, Mariah?"

Mariah stopped and looked down at him. "He was a very good man. Why do you say so?"

"Because you're a very good woman."

Rowan closed his eyes and turned away to slumber. Though his body was weak, something sparked in his spirit that morning. At the table of a courageous old woman and in the company of a gallant young woman, Rowan began to heal, and the call of the Prince began to sound…a call to something noble…and he could think of nothing more noble than the mission of the Resolutes.

ELEVEN

MYSTERIOUS KNIGHT

Rowan awoke to a dreadful realization. He got out of bed as quickly as he could, stumbled to the door, and opened it.

"Mariah!" he called, but no one answered.

"Mariah!" he called again.

He heard the back door open, and Mariah appeared at the end of the hallway with a basketful of greens and vegetables. She dropped the basket and hurried to Rowan's bedchamber, sensing his concern.

"What is it, Rowan?" She offered a shoulder of support.

He shook his head. "How long have I been sleeping?"

"Two hours…perhaps three. Why?"

Zetta was now coming down the hallway.

"We have to leave here immediately," he said.

"Why, Rowan? What's wrong?"

"All of us are in danger. Balenteen knew that Sir Aldwyn was my friend. I'm sure he'll think to have the sentinels investigate his home. I'm surprised they're not here already."

Mariah's eyes opened wide. "I'll gather our things," she said—but it was too late.

They all froze at the sound of heavy boots on the kitchen floor-boards. A moment later, a massive figure appeared at the end of the hallway. Though he did not wear a sentinel's uniform, Rowan was certain he was a leader of the sentinel force. His black leather armor was festooned with bright silver markings. He stood even taller than Rowan, with a physique as muscular as Rowan's had been during his tournament days. Dark brown hair was pulled back in a short braid at the back of his head, highlighting his olive skin, prominent nose, and jaw line. His hand rested on the pommel of his sword, and his stance nearly spanned the entire hallway.

"Where is Sir Aldwyn?" The man's voice was urgent, his countenance fierce as he glared at the trio in the hallway.

Rowan stood as straight as he could and stepped past Mariah and Zetta. "I am the one you have come for. Leave them alone," he said with as much authority as he could muster.

The mighty knight's eyes narrowed as he strolled toward Rowan. He came within inches of his face, gazing into Rowan's eyes with fire in his own. He reached up and grabbed Rowan's neck just below his jaw. Rowan tried to pull away, but he was powerless in the man's iron grip. Mariah tried to come to Rowan's aid, but the man just held her at arm's length while she clawed at his arm.

Surprisingly, the man did not squeeze or attempt to strangle Rowan. Instead, he slowly turned Rowan's head from one side to the other, as if inspecting him. Rowan held up a hand to tell Mariah to back away, and she halted her fruitless attempt at help. The man looked down at Rowan's frail form and sneered.

"Impossible! You are not the one." His voice was thick with indignation. He dropped his hand back to his sword. "Where is Aldwyn?"

Just then the front door of the home exploded inward in a shower of splinters. Rowan, Mariah, and Zetta stood dumbfounded at the sound of many armed men bursting into the front parlor.

"Sentinels!" whispered Zetta with alarm in her eyes.

The large, mysterious knight responded in the blink of an eye. He drew his sword and rushed down the hallway toward the intruders. Aldwyn's home was instantly filled with crashing swords, overturned tables, and broken pottery. It seemed an impossible fight, for the knight was clearly outmanned. Rowan wasn't sure who he hoped would win, for either victor seemed a threat.

Zetta urged Mariah and Rowan to retreat with her into the bed-chamber, where they locked the door. Rowan quickly donned his boots and jacket.

"What should we do?" Mariah asked, but Rowan just shook his head. This chamber had no windows.

"Help me move the bed," Zetta said. "Here." She tugged at the frame. "Against the door."

Rowan and Mariah looked at each other. "That won't hold them long."

She shook her head. "Come—we haven't much time."

The ruckus in the home sounded as if the entire place was being destroyed.

They slid the bed up against the door.

"There," Zetta pointed at a rug that had been covered by the bed.

Mariah knelt down and lifted the rug to reveal a trapdoor. She looked up at Rowan and smiled.

"Each of the bedrooms has one," Zetta said. "Sir Aldwyn had them dug last year. They lead to the stables in the back.

Rowan knelt down to help lift the door, but he knew that Mariah was bearing most of the burden. Just as the trapdoor was laid back on the floor, the ruckus outside their room stopped.

"Hurry!" Rowan said to Zetta.

Someone tried to open the door to the room, but it hit against the bed. Rowan froze as he realized it would be impossible for them to make it through the trapdoor in time. He looked about for a weapon as the door was forced open, sliding the bed across the floor.

"Come out!" the deep voice of the mysterious knight ordered. He stood as broad as the doorway.

"Who are you?" Rowan asked.

"I am a Knight of the Prince. Come out! We haven't much time. Soon they will be back with reinforcements." The knight kept his sword at ready while he lifted the bed with one hand and turned it on its side to clear the doorway. He motioned for the three of them to follow him.

Mariah and Zetta looked at Rowan, who shrugged and nodded. He still didn't trust the knight, but what choice did they have? They followed the knight down the hall into a scene of utter chaos. Chairs were overturned, lanterns broken, walls slashed, and eight sentinels lay dead, sprawled across furniture and floorboards.

Rowan looked at the knight and marveled. The scene reminded him a bit of the day he was captured, but he definitely preferred this outcome.

The knight led them out to Aldwyn's stables. Once there, he turned and glared at them. "It is paramount that I find Sir Aldwyn."

"Why should we believe you?" Rowan asked.

The man hesitated. "I am Sir Lijah of Chessington. I am on a mission, and I was told that Sir Aldwyn could help me."

Zetta threw a shawl over her shoulders, then walked up to the man and stared into his eyes. After a moment of strange silence, she turned and looked at Rowan and Mariah. "I believe him. I will take him to Sir Aldwyn."

Zetta turned to Rowan. "I'm afraid you wouldn't survive the journey." She looked up to the Boundary Mountains, then back to Rowan and Mariah. If they were going to the mountains, Rowan knew she was right.

Zetta put a hand on Mariah's arm. "When he is strong enough, come to the kingdom's first sun. You will find us there."

"No." Rowan tried to stand tall and look strong. "Mariah is going with you."

Mariah looked at Rowan and opened her mouth to protest, but Rowan grabbed her shoulders.

"You have already done more for me than you should have. You may find your father and your brother up there, and I'll not stand in the way of that." Rowan smiled at her. "Go with them. I know of a place here where I can rest and recover."

Mariah's eyes softened. For the first time since they'd met, Rowan saw tenderness for him beyond just that of a nursemaid, and it warmed his heart. Perhaps in another time or place, their lives might have crossed with a more fortuitous outcome, but here in the midst of rising tyranny and impending war, it would not be so.

Mariah lifted a gentle hand to his gaunt cheek, then turned and helped Lijah tack up the horses. When all was ready, she handed Sierra's reins to Rowan and mounted up with Zetta and Lijah. Sir Lijah hurried their departure, and Rowan saluted his good-bye. With tremendous effort, Rowan managed to climb onto Sierra's saddle. He looked toward Mariah and saw that she was looking back at him once more. He waved, then trotted Sierra out of sight behind the stables and stopped. He leaned forward onto Sierra's neck and waited…waited for the next wave of sentinels to come. There simply wasn't enough life in his body to go on.

Random regrets flitted through Rowan's mind as he sat there. The marauders had indeed killed him in the end, for he was just a shell of a man with no hope of becoming anything more. Any prison in Laos would have to be better than the cave prison of the marauders, he reckoned. He wondered how different his life would be today if he hadn't let arrogance and the appeal of fame and fortune draw him into their net.

After a few long moments, he heard a galloping horse approaching and didn't care. The horse and rider flew around the corner of the stables. The steed whinnied as the rider pulled it in.

"You are a very poor liar, Rowan," Mariah said. "You have nowhere to go except with me."

Rowan slowly sat up and turned around in his saddle.

"That obvious?" he asked.

Mariah nodded. "Come on. Let's get out of here." She kicked her horse, and Rowan followed.

TWELVE

BANDITS

 They moved as quickly as Rowan could go to get out and away from Laos. Once they felt safe, their pace slowed significantly. It took Mariah nearly five days to get Rowan back to the farm. The journey to Laos, the turmoil while there, and the return trip to the farm had taken a significant toll on him.

For a while, his condition was almost as bad as when Mariah had first discovered him in the cave. This time, however, Mariah was obstinate about what Rowan could and could not do until he was healthy again. The process was long and slow, but Mariah was a faithful caregiver. After two months, Rowan began to look like a thin but normal man again. After four, he began purposefully to rebuild his muscles and was able to help with some of the duties required to keep the farm going.

Each day that passed, Rowan grew stronger and stronger, as did his affection for the one who had saved his life…twice. He was careful to allow Mariah room to live without feeling any pressure to become emotionally connected to him. She seemed to appreciate this about Rowan, for the loss of her husband was still a wound he knew she felt deeply.

Twice he had passed by her bedchamber on his way to the outbuilding for the evening and heard her softly weeping. The second time he knocked and carefully opened the door to find her sitting on her bed holding Palson's shirt in her lap.

"Are you all right, Mariah?" he asked gently.

She nodded.

Rowan slowly closed the door and left her to her memories.

When harvest season came, Rowan went to the fields with Mariah, and together they brought in a bountiful crop, considering the small size of the farm. It felt good for Rowan to work hard and feel stronger the next day instead of weaker. At last he had finally crested the recovery peak.

Rowan and Mariah talked often of the events in Cameria. The small village nearby provided some news of regional events, but not enough to satisfy them. Rowan felt torn between the simple life of the farm and the knowledge that Cameria was slowly being conquered from both within and without by foreign enemies. His return to Laos was inevitable. When he did return, he wanted to be prepared.

One day late in the fall, five months after they had returned from Laos, Rowan was chopping wood in a nearby grove of trees to prepare for winter. The ax felt good in his hands, and it reminded him of his nearly forgotten sword. He finished chopping the wood and began loading the cart, wondering just how much of a load Mariah's old workhorse, Biscuit, could haul up the rise and back to the house.

Just then Rowan heard Mariah scream, and he sprinted toward home.

"Rowa—!" she called out, but this cry was cut short.

When he broke from the trees, he could see two strange horses tethered near the front of the house. Two men were pilfering Mariah's home, and she was doing her best to stop them—with little success. Rowan chastised himself for not grabbing the ax before leaving the cart, but now it was too late to turn back.

"Back off, woman." One of the men struck Mariah across the face, then threw her up against the side of the home. He passed through the door for another trip to the food pantry. The second bandit was tying produce and goods to his horse—essentials that Rowan and Mariah had worked hard to harvest and trade for. He looked up and saw Rowan approach.

"Wallen! We got comp'ny!" the man shouted back over his shoulder as he drew his sword. Then he turned toward Rowan. "Stay back, and no one will die t'day."

The other thief hurried out the door toward the horses with one arm full of booty and the other holding a sword. Rowan saw Mariah duck into the house behind him.

Rowan slowed his approach. "No one has to die today as long as you put everything back and ride away."

The two men looked at each other and started to laugh. "We're the ones wit' the swords, an' besides, if'n you did 'ave one, a farmer's no fighter. Now back off!"

The larger of the two thugs jabbed his sword at Rowan to get him away from their horses.

"You don't seem to understand," Rowan said calmly as Mariah moved up quietly behind the men.

The thugs hesitated. Just then a sword flew over their heads from behind them, and Rowan snatched it out of midair. "I do have a sword," he said, "and I am not a farmer."

Rowan engaged both men simultaneously. It took him a few strokes to find his rhythm and the feel of the sword, but soon he had both men in steady retreat. They began to panic as his mastery was revealed. At one point Rowan parried, feigned a thrust, and sliced across the sword arm of the larger thug. He screamed, backed away, and cradled his bleeding wound.

"That's for striking the lady," Rowan said to the man.

The other man hesitated with eyes wide.

"This next one's for stealing," Rowan taunted.

The man threw his sword down and backed away with his hands up.

"You, there," Rowan said to the larger bandit. "Drop your sword."

The man dropped it. Rowan maneuvered the men back to their horses. "Put it all back exactly where you found it. Mariah, fetch a cloth."

Mariah looked at Rowan as if he'd lost his mind. He winked. "We don't want him bleeding all over the floor, now do we?"

Rowan and Mariah waited while one thief tied a bandage around the other's arm and both thieves became busy returning all of the stolen goods back to the house. The men looked quite humiliated during the task, but Rowan was not done with them. On their last trip, Rowan took their horses and tied them up on the far side of the home.

"Hey, where's our horses?" the larger brute said with a scowl on his face when they exited the home.

"You will have your horses back when you're finished paying for your crime," Rowan answered. "Down in that grove of trees you will find cut wood, an old mare, and a cart. Load up the cart with the wood; then bring it back and stack the wood neatly alongside the house on the south side."

The men sneered and hesitated. Rowan stepped toward them with his sword ready. "Hurry along now, before I feel like using this again."

The men ducked their heads and started toward the trees. Rowan could hear them grumbling at each other as they went.

"Having fun?" Mariah came to stand beside Rowan.

Rowan just smiled as he watched the men disappear into the trees.

"I didn't know if you remembered how to use a sword after all these months," she said. "I guess you must have been pretty good after all," she teased.

Rowan lifted up the sword and saw the mark of the Prince in the pommel. "It's a beautiful sword," he said. "Where did you get it?"

"My father has three more in a trunk in my bedchamber. He believes in being prepared."

"I'm glad for it," Rowan said, "and for your quick thinking. I don't know what—" Rowan looked down at Mariah and saw the cut and bruise on her forehead from the brute's attack. He reached up and gently pushed her hair away from the injury to inspect it more closely. "You're bleeding."

Mariah shrugged. "It's nothing."

"Come." Rowan took her hand and led her to the well. He drew a bucket of cold water, then dampened a clean cloth and gently cleaned the blood away. He held the cool cloth on the bruise.

Mariah looked up at him. "Thank you."

"I have a long way to go to catch up to you," he said. "But I'm willing to stick around and try if you'll let me."

Mariah smiled briefly, then turned away and looked toward the trees where the would-be robbers were working.

"Should we feed them?" she asked.

Rowan was stunned by her question—and by this glimpse into the beauty of her heart.

"I reckon that would be the princely thing to do," he replied.

Rowan watched the two men closely as they stacked the wood beside the house, making sure they did the job with excellence. When they were finished, they looked like whipped puppies begging to be let go.

"I have one more task for you two before you leave," Rowan said.

"Look, mister," the bigger brute said, "we're real sorry we tried to steal your food."

"Yes, I'm sure you are," Rowan said with a smirk.

"And we promise never ta bother you nor the lady agin," the smaller fellow added.

"That would be wise since if you do, you'll have more than an arm to bandage," Rowan said. "Now, go to the well and clean up. Lady Mariah is preparing a delicious meal for us to enjoy."

The two men looked at each other in astonishment. They started toward the well, but Rowan held up his sword as a gate to stop them.

"I expect you'll be very polite to Lady Mariah and have good manners at the table," he said solemnly.

"Yes sir," the men replied.

By the end of the day, Wallen and Wilbur had eaten a satisfying dinner and heard the life-changing story of the Prince. They left as changed men…with an invitation to come back and hear more.

That evening, as Rowan passed Mariah's open door on his way to the outbuilding where he slept, he found her kneeling over a trunk on the floor.

"How's that forehead?" He leaned against the doorpost.

She turned her head and stared at him but said nothing. She then turned back to the trunk. She lifted something from her lap, and only then did Rowan realize what it was. Mariah gently laid Palson's folded shirt into the trunk and closed the lid.

"I'm sorry." Rowan felt like an intruder. He quietly turned on his heel and left.

He went to the outbuilding and began gathering his few belongings—mostly clothing Mariah had given him. Though he was not yet to full strength, today was evidence that he did not need Mariah's care anymore. In an instant his presence around her home had become extremely awkward, and he knew it was time to leave.

He went to the stables and began saddling Biscuit. Before long, Mariah came and leaned on a post nearby. Rowan glanced over at her and continued to work as he talked.

"You've strengthened me and brought me back in more ways than you'll ever know, and for that I will be eternally grateful. Today I realized that I am not here because I need your help anymore. I'm here because…" Rowan stopped and looked at Mariah. "It's just time for me to leave." He fiddled with the tack as he added, "I'll need the horse to get to the village, but I'll get another one somehow and send Biscuit back to you."

Mariah came to stand in front of him. As she looked up, he gazed into her eyes and was captivated by them once again.

"Palson was indeed a good man," Mariah said. She reached out and put her hand on his arm. "And so are you, Rowan. You too have strengthened and healed me in ways you'll never know. I don't want you to leave."

Rowan looked down into blue eyes that were clearly welcoming him into her life. "Are you sure, Mariah?"

She gently smiled and nodded. "I'm sure."

He reached down, lifted her hand, and gently kissed it. "I am not worthy of you, Mariah, but I promise to endeavor to be so for the rest of my life."

Mariah smiled at Rowan in a way that made him feel as if he could single-handedly defeat an entire legion of Shadow Warriors for the Prince.

That day Rowan and Mariah pledged their love for each other. Over the next few weeks, Rowan and Mariah's courtship affirmed their hearts for each other, and they made arrangements to be married in the village. There was no dancing or feast, no gala parade, just two hearts that quietly chose to love each other and to live their lives one for the other.

THE RESOLUTES

 With each passing month, Rowan grew stronger. He trained daily with the sword, and Mariah joined him to take up where she had left off with her father years earlier. Their love grew into a true partnership: Mariah completed Rowan, and he completed her.

They spent a happy winter in the cozy comfort of their farmhouse, the joy of their new love touched only by troubling reports about more changes in Laos and the other cities of Cameria. Rowan returned from hunting one spring morning to see a neighbor from the village cantering away from the house. Mariah waited for him at the door, a worried expression on her face.

"Nora had news," she told him, her eyes filled with anguish. "It's just as we feared. The Knights of the Prince have been banned in Krowen." Her face crumpled as she added, "The haven has been closed, the leaders arrested. Oh, Rowan…"

Rowan pulled her to him, his heart heavy. "I was afraid this was coming," he said. "Laos will be next."

He felt her nod against his chest. She sniffled heavily, then pulled back enough to look him in the eye. "It's time, Rowan."

He took a deep breath. "I know. We'll talk to Reginald tomorrow and work out something about the farm."

The decision was made in an instant, but it had been brewing all that winter. Many long evenings by the fire, while sleet scratched against the windowpanes, they had talked of finding Mariah's father and brother and of joining the cause of the Resolutes. As isolated as they were, news still kept trickling in of disturbing developments in the cities. And though part of them longed to remain isolated from the cares of the rest of Cameria and enjoy their quiet life a little longer, their hearts could not turn away from the cries of the oppressed. Good people were suffering and possibly dying, and both Rowan and Mariah felt called to do everything in their power to stop it.

For months now, they had known it was just a matter of time before they left. Now they both knew the moment had come.

Within a week, they had boarded up the farmhouse, entrusted the remaining animals to neighbors, and packed enough provisions to last for several weeks of travel. With two riding horses and a pack horse, they set out east. They made a point to bypass Laos, for there was no need to enter it and risk being imprisoned. After a two days' ride, they found themselves drawing near to the Boundary Mountains, where Zetta had said the Resolutes were camped.

But where in the Boundary Mountains were they?

"When he is strong enough," the old woman had said, "come to the kingdom's first sun." But what did that mean?

"The sun rises in the east and first strikes the highest peaks of the Boundary Mountains," Rowan mused.

"Yes, and Zetta looked southeast of Laos when she said it." Mariah pointed. "That's where Thunder Mountain is."

The peak of Thunder Mountain pierced the sky just to their northeast. The mountain was only one of many in the seemingly endless range that ran from one end of the kingdom to the other, but they considered it their best shot.

The mountain wasn't so uniformly steep that they couldn't navigate it with their horses, but it still took them three days of hard climbing to reach the lofty tree line. The air was thin and cold here, and they decided that the Resolutes surely would not have made their base higher than this. They could see the city of Laos far below them and thought how unthreatening it seemed from here. They combed the western face of the mountain another three days, but could find no trace of the resistance forces.

One morning as they were trying to shake the chill from their bones by huddling around a small campfire, Mariah leaned into Rowan, and he placed his arm around her shivering shoulders.

"It's a shame we don't have a little sun on this side of the mountain to warm us in the morning," Rowan said.

Mariah nodded, then slowly looked up at Rowan with a countenance of illumination. Then Rowan realized it too and shook his head in disgust. "We've been searching on the wrong side of the mountain!"

They laughed at themselves, but the revelation warmed and motivated them. They quickly broke camp and started their trek to the eastern face of Thunder Mountain...where the sun first struck the kingdom.

They finally arrived on the edge of a beautiful, lofty mountain plateau where the snow melted into ice-cold streams. Green grass and vibrant wildflowers shared the landscape with evergreens and deciduous trees bursting forth with new life. They dismounted for a short break, long enough to marvel at the beauty of it all.

"From up here, it seems as though everything is right in the kingdom," Mariah said with a radiant smile across her face.

Rowan looked at her and nodded. "As long as we're together, I think it shall be."

Mariah put her arm through his and squeezed, then froze. "Did you see that?"

"See what?" Rowan followed her eyes, looking just ahead of them to where the trees became thicker.

"I'm not sure, but something moved up there—perhaps a deer or a mountain goat, but something moved."

"Stay here." Rowan handed the reins of his horse to Mariah. "I'll take a look."

He drew his sword and walked about thirty steps toward the trees.

"Drop your sword!" Rowan heard a voice shout from the protection of the trees and underbrush.

"Who goes there?" Rowan replied, sword ready.

"Drop your sword now!" the voice said again.

Rowan hesitated. "I will not. Show yourself."

Three men exited the trees with swords drawn and surrounded him.

"The work of One saves many," Rowan said.

"You have one last chance to drop your sword," the leader said solemnly. Despite the odds, his voice was less confident now that he realized he was facing a foe much larger than himself.

"Tell me who you are, and I will consider it," Rowan replied.

The leader made the first move, but based on the man's stance and sword placement, Rowan knew exactly what it would be and beat him to it. A parry and a powerful bind left the leader swordless and speechless. Rowan didn't wait for the other two to advance. His sword flew like lightning to engage them, and they were so overwhelmed with Rowan's powerful and quick cuts that they fell into steady retreat until one stumbled backward onto the ground. The third man had the look of panic on his face as Rowan brought his blade to bear singly upon him. In three strokes the man's sword was lying on the ground and his arms were in the air.

Then five more men exited the trees and surrounded Rowan. The leader recovered his sword, embarrassment still stinging red in his cheeks.

Rowan paused to prepare himself, quickly analyzing each man's stance, position, and the surrounding terrain. He reveled in the thrill of a sword fight, and he didn't care if there were five or fifty. Every fiber of his body seemed to exist for this.

They all prepared for the encounter, but then Mariah stepped between two of the men and into the circle of swords. This stunned everyone, including Rowan. She didn't draw her sword or even seem the least bit alarmed. She went to Rowan and placed a gentle hand on his sword arm.

"If you wound them all," she said with a sweet smile, "we will never be taken to their camp."

Rowan snorted, stood straight, and sheathed his sword. The others stared at him as if unsure whether to relax or attack.

Mariah turned about to face the leader. "Good sir, I am Mariah, and I am looking for my father, Sir Fairchild of Berwick. This is Sir Rowan, friend of Sir Aldwyn. Can you help us find them?"

The leader lowered his sword. "Perhaps, my lady. Please come with me."

The rest of the men relaxed their swords and seemed relieved to do so. Mariah turned back to Rowan. "Sometimes a few polite words and a smile can be stronger than a sword," she said with a wink.

Rowan huffed. "You, my lovely wife, will always have an advantage over me in that regard."

The leader spoke briefly to one of the men, who promptly found his horse and galloped off. Very little was said as they waited, and the men seemed reluctant to become too unguarded around Rowan after having seen his skill with the sword. Following a lengthy delay, the sound of two galloping horses filtered through the woods and then burst into the open. One of the men jumped from his horse the instant he saw Mariah.

"Julian!" Mariah exclaimed as they embraced.

At that, the leader of the men guarding them relaxed and ordered all to return to their lookouts.

Mariah and her brother stepped back and held each other's arms for a moment, joy filling their eyes.

"Is father…?" Mariah seemed hesitant to finish her question.

"Father is fine, Mariah," Julian said with a wide grin. "He is meeting with the leaders of another encampment but should be back tonight."

Mariah took a deep, satisfied breath.

Julian quickly scanned his surroundings, his eyes coming to rest on Rowan.

"Where is Palson?" he asked.

Mariah's joyful countenance immediately vanished.

"Sister, what has happened?"

"He…he died, Julian."

Julian was speechless for a moment, and then took Mariah into his arms once more. "I'm so sorry, and we left you alone. How long ago?"

"Just two months after you and Father left."

"That long ago? Why didn't you come for us?"

"It's a long story, best left for both you and Father to hear together." Mariah turned to Rowan. "Julian this is Sir Rowan of Laos. He…helped me find you."

Julian looked up at Rowan and nodded. "I am grateful to you, sir."

Rowan nodded in return. Obviously Mariah wasn't ready to tell Julian everything quite yet.

"He is a friend of Sir Aldwyn," Mariah told her brother. "Do you know of him?"

"If you're a friend of Sir Aldwyn, then you're a friend of mine," Julian said. "I can take you to him."

"I'd be grateful," Rowan said with a nod.

Julian turned back to Mariah. "It is so good to see you, sister. Come, I have much to show you."

Julian led Mariah and Rowan back through the trees. "We must be extremely careful these days," he said. "Our pass code was compromised a few months ago."

They traveled across the plateau and through a large wooded area. Then they crested a knoll that opened up to a shallow valley. Rowan and Mariah stood dumbfounded as they beheld a settlement that was as large as a city.

"The Resolutes," Julian said, staring out over the valley. "At least, *one* of our encampments. We call it Eagle's Nest."

The settlement flowed up and down the valley for miles, with tents and other temporary structures mixed in with more permanent buildings and huts. Sections of rock wall offered some measure of cover on one side. Higher up, where the valley met the steeper slopes of the mountain, the dwellings meshed right into naturally formed caves. The melting snows formed a river that meandered down through the middle of the settlement and disappeared far down the valley.

"So many," Mariah said softly.

"Yes," Julian said. "There are more than fourteen thousand of us at last count, and we continue to grow. There are more encampments in other parts of the Boundary Mountains as well, but we are the largest as far as we know."

Rowan just shook his head, hardly believing what he was seeing. What was happening to cause such a thing?

"Are they all Knights of the Prince?" Rowan asked.

"Mostly, but not all," Julian replied. "All who oppose the oppression of our freedom to follow the Prince, or any other order for that matter, are welcome."

"Aren't you concerned about being discovered?" he asked. "Why aren't there more men on guard?"

Julian smiled. "On our journey here we passed more than two hundred armed men. You just didn't see them. There are fifty men just behind those rock walls who would have been mounted and upon us in a moment if I had not signaled. Except for the smaller children, all fourteen thousand of us are armed and ready to fight at the blast of the warning trumpet. You needn't worry about our readiness, Sir Rowan."

Julian pointed to what looked like a training area for young knights.

"Sir Aldwyn is just over there. He has trained thousands of knights in preparation for the battle. He's very good at it."

"Battle?" Rowan asked.

Julian looked soberly at Rowan and Mariah.

"As I'm sure you know, Cameria is not what it once was. The freedom we once enjoyed has vanished, especially in the cities, and the oppression of Lord Gavaah is steadily growing."

"Gavaah?" Rowan stared at him, bewildered. "The Camerian Tournament Council president?"

"He is much more than that," Julian said. "He is now ruler of the United Cities, but we believe he is being supported by sources outside the region. These are dark days for Cameria, and we must do something to change what is happening before it's too late."

Julian kicked his horse, and Rowan and Mariah followed him into the camp of the Resolutes. Looking around at the crowds of people living in spartan circumstances, Rowan marveled at the commitment of these people…people who had come from all across the region to join the cause. There are pivotal times in the life of a city, a region, and even a kingdom that will be determined by the actions or inaction of the people who abide within them. Rowan knew he was witnessing such a time and that he was now an inseparable part of it.

Stirred by the momentum of fourteen thousand noble people on a mountaintop overlooking the kingdom, Rowan remembered the words of the Prince from a long-ago dream. *Your life is not over, for you are a mighty knight of the King. Time is short, and I have a mission that awaits you.*

"Surely this is it," he whispered to himself. "How can there be a greater mission than to bring liberty to the great land of Cameria and her people?"

FOURTEEN

FLIGHT OF THE EAGLE

 Julian brought Rowan and Mariah to the training grounds of Eagle's Nest, where Sir Aldwyn was occupied with the task of managing the training of over five hundred men, women, and youths. As they approached, Aldwyn was meeting with fourteen trainers and giving instructions for the day. He looked up and stopped midsentence, fastening a stunned gaze on Rowan. When he didn't continue, the trainers all turned and looked at Rowan and Mariah too.

"That is all for now," Aldwyn finally managed. "Dismissed."

Rowan dismounted and walked toward Aldwyn through the stream of dispersing knights. Aldwyn just stood and stared.

"Rowan?" he finally asked.

Rowan just nodded, not sure what sort of greeting his mentor would give him.

"Rowan?" Aldwyn asked again. This time he started walking toward him.

"It is I, Sir Aldwyn," Rowan said.

At that, Aldwyn quickened his pace to close the distance between them. His mouth hung open in an expression of utter disbelief.

Rowan put out an arm of greeting, but Aldwyn pushed past it and threw his arms around him. Rowan returned the embrace, his heart warmed by the gesture.

Aldwyn stepped back but did not let loose of Rowan. His eyes shone with joy as he realized that his protégé was indeed alive and standing before him.

"Please forgive me, Sir Aldwyn. I was such a fool." Rowan hadn't expected to feel such strong emotions wash over him as he stood before the man who had dedicated a portion of his life to lift a poor street urchin out of the gutter. His eyes welled up.

Aldwyn put a hand to Rowan's face. "Thank the King you are alive, my son."

Son? Aldwyn considered him his son? Rowan lowered his gaze to the ground, thinking how little he deserved that title.

Aldwyn embraced him once more, then put an arm around him to lead him away. "We have much to talk about…and prepare for," Aldwyn said.

"Wait," Rowan motioned to Mariah, who still sat patiently on her horse beside Julian. "There's someone I'd like you to meet."

Mariah and Julian dismounted as Rowan and Aldwyn approached.

"Sir Aldwyn, I'd like you to meet…Lady Mariah." Rowan looked questioningly at her.

"It's all right," she said with a smile. "I've just told Julian."

Julian smiled sheepishly as Rowan finished his introduction. "My wife."

Aldwyn's eyes lifted; then a wide grin crossed his face. He took Mariah's hand and bowed low to kiss it. "I am honored, my lady. Now I see and understand why Rowan's eyes glow with joy."

"Rowan speaks nothing but great admiration for you, good sir," Mariah replied. "I am pleased to meet you."

Aldwyn invited them into the training cabin and offered them food and drink. Rowan looked in wonder at the collection of arms stacked neatly in the corners of the cabin.

"What's happening here, Aldwyn?" Rowan asked once they were settled around a table. "Are things truly so bad in Laos that this is necessary?"

"Lord Gavaah rules Cameria," Aldwyn said soberly. "And each day his grip becomes tighter and tighter. He has commandeered the people's homes and land, banned all orders of knights except those that accept his new statutes, and imprisoned anyone opposing his authority. Those who remain and abide under his rule have been lulled into believing that his control is for their own good, but those who love freedom and recognize what he is doing are willing to fight against him."

"You've seen this coming for a long time, haven't you?" Rowan asked.

The older man nodded. "I tried to tell you, but you were... preoccupied."

Rowan dropped his eyes, embarrassed again by who he had been.

Aldwyn laid a hand on his shoulder. "I had no idea, however, that Gavaah was behind the changes...or that his influence would expand so quickly." He took a sip of his warm drink. "But what is happening in Laos is just one of many, Rowan."

Aldwyn paused to look at Mariah and Julian. Julian was nodding. "This is really all about Chessington. Gavaah is just a pawn of Lord Malizimar, and Malizimar of Lucius himself. We've heard disturbing news of another tyrant rising to power within Chessington—a man by the name of Alexander Histen."

Aldwyn paused to see if the name meant anything to Rowan. When Rowan looked at him blankly, he went on. "We know almost nothing about Histen, but from the reports we are getting, he is a charismatic leader who is more dangerous than ten Lord Gavaahs. His influence in the kingdom is spreading quickly. And with Gavaah ruling Cameria, Chessington is getting almost no support, so its citizens' ability to fight back against Histen has nearly been eliminated."

Rowan and Mariah looked at each other with grave concern showing on their faces.

"We've come to join you and your cause." Rowan reached across the table to hold Mariah's hand. "We will fight for Cameria and its freedom."

"We are grateful to have you," Aldwyn said sincerely. "Now your sword will fly for something of true value."

"What plans are being made?" Mariah asked.

"I'm not at liberty to say just yet," Aldwyn said. "Come to the council meeting tomorrow. Sir Whitley will be announcing our plan, or at least a portion of it."

Rowan's reunion with Sir Aldwyn was both sweet and foreboding, for the news of conditions in his home region was extremely disturbing. Only now did Rowan fully appreciate the freedoms he had once enjoyed and had now lost.

By late afternoon, news that the former Laos tournament champion had joined the Resolutes spread quickly throughout the encampment and bolstered the morale of the people there. Though it had now been nearly two years since his tournament days, Rowan's fame had evidently not diminished, nor had his favor with the people. He was actually quite embarrassed by all the attention he received, since the tournaments seemed like frivolous entertainment compared to the significant actions the people were taking here. He considered them the true heroes now, and he said so. But after his first few fumbled attempts to express his humility, Mariah helped him turn the praise they gave him to the Prince, and he was grateful to her for the help.

That evening, after Julian had arranged a place for Rowan and Mariah to stay, Mariah's father returned from his mission. Sir Fairchild was a tall man with hair as dark as Mariah's, though his was in the process of turning white at the temples. He was a distinguished-looking knight, but his dignity softened into delight when he caught sight of his daughter. After a tearful reunion, Sir Fairchild welcomed Rowan into the family as a son.

The next day, Rowan and Mariah followed Julian and Fairchild up the valley to the point on the mountain where the caves began.

"Where are we going, Father?" Mariah asked.

"I want to show you something quite remarkable," he said with a smile.

They entered a part of the encampment that was significantly different from where they had been. Two buildings and seven large tents buzzed with frenetic activity. A variety of tall structures had been constructed from wood, steel, and rope for a purpose Rowan couldn't possibly imagine.

He and his comrades ducked through one tent to see dozens of men and women working fervently on a strange-looking apparatus. The four visitors walked toward a large table where three men were bent over, examining sheets of vellum full of sketches and notes.

"Sir Scott," Fairchild called.

The men he addressed seemed lost in thought and conversation, oblivious to Fairchild's call or the group's approach. One of the men finally jabbed and pointed, and a spry young man looked up, running his hand through wavy reddish hair.

"Sir Fairchild," he said with a broad grin. "I didn't see you come in."

"You never do," Fairchild said with a wink toward Rowan and Mariah that Sir Scott totally missed because he had turned away to make a mark on the vellum with a quill.

"What can I do for you?" Sir Scott asked when he turned back around.

"I'd like you to meet my daughter, Mariah, and her husband, Sir Rowan," Fairchild said.

Sir Scott came toward them and extended a hand. "I'm pleased to meet—"

"*The* Sir Rowan?" one of the other men exclaimed, interrupting Sir Scott. The man came straight for Rowan with eyes wide, holding out his hand.

"I'm not sure what you mean by that, sir," Rowan asked, wishing the man didn't mean what he knew he did.

"Sir Rowan, tournament champion of Laos? The one presumed dead?" This fellow was taller than Scott and a bit huskier, with a fringe of dark brown hair. He shook Rowan's hand with enthusiasm.

Rowan hung his head sheepishly. "I did fight in the tournaments—"

"He's the one." Mariah stuck out her hand while casting a sly grin back at her husband.

Sir Fairchild looked at Rowan with a new measure of respect, then back to Sir Scott's colleague. "I didn't know you followed the games so closely, Sir John."

"I thought everyone did," John replied incredulously. "Everyone knew of the great Sir Rowan."

Rowan shook his head. "That's not what I—"

"Jeffrey," John reached back and nudged the third man, who was still hunched over the vellums. "Get your head out of that drawing and come meet Sir Rowan…and his wife. Our younger brother lives in a different world sometimes," John said with a smirk.

Rowan nearly laughed but caught himself. From his perspective, all three of them seemed to live in a different world.

The third fellow, a very young man with a slender build and a mop of white blond hair, stood straight and came to greet them. He was quiet, hardly uttering a word, and he didn't seem to care much about Rowan's fame—which annoyed Sir John and comforted Rowan. He shook Rowan's hand, his eyes narrowing as he scrutinized him up and down.

"We'll have to increase the span and thicken the spars for this one," he said.

Sir Scott nodded. "Yes…could be a bit of a challenge. More tests will have to be run."

Rowan looked at Mariah, and she shared his perplexed look.

An amused smile played on Fairchild's face. "Sir Scott, would you mind explaining your work to Rowan and Mariah?"

Sir John grabbed Rowan's shoulder. "We'll do better than that. We'll *show* them. We're just about ready to make our maiden voyage…with a real rider!"

Now Rowan was really confused, but intrigued. He and Mariah followed John, Scott, and Jeffrey through the tent and into a small field where the valley dropped quickly away before flattening out again far below them. A large wooden platform had been built at the edge of the drop-off, and sitting on the platform was the strangest object Rowan had seen in his entire life. Two men and a young woman were making adjustments to an unwieldy-looking triangular structure made of wood and some kind of thin sheeting. It rested atop three supports. Below it hung a wooden bar and a leather harness. On the ground near the base of the wooden platform, a team of people fussed over an individual wearing leather armor and a tight-fitting helmet, who seemed quite annoyed at all the attention. As they approached, Rowan noted the excitement in the people's voices.

"Are you sure you're up for this?" a young woman as tall as Mariah asked the suited individual. "It's not too late to back out, Annie."

"Of course I'm up for it," a determined female voice replied from beneath the helmet. "Let's get on with it."

"How are we doing, Dyanne?" Sir Scott asked the tall woman. At the sound of his voice, she turned to greet them.

"All is set," she said with a sly grin, "including the rider."

"Sir Rowan…Lady Mariah, please meet our sisters. Lady Dyanne," he motioned toward the tall woman. "Lady Elizabeth," Scott motioned up toward the platform, where a thin, dark-haired woman waved down toward them and then turned back to check the sheeting on the wing one more time. "And Lady Anne"—he nodded toward the suited woman—"the only one light enough…and gutsy enough…to ride our first wing."

With hands on her leather-clad hips, Lady Anne nodded and shot them a quick smile.

"What is this?" Rowan finally asked, gesturing to the big triangle.

"This, Sir Rowan, is a glider," Scott said with pride. "Jeffrey?" Scott turned to his younger brother, who held up a smaller model of the wing structure on the platform. It was about as long as his forearm.

"Watch," he said, and he walked to the edge of the drop-off, where he gave the glider model a gentle push. It swooped downward at first, then glided in a beautifully smooth trajectory toward the valley.

Rowan's eyes widened as he began to understand what was happening here. He looked back up at the wing and then down at the rider.

"You are going to—" He couldn't finish the sentence because it seemed so absurd.

"Exactly!" Sir John said with a grin. "We tested it with weights similar to a person, but this is our first time with a rider."

Rowan couldn't believe what he was seeing and hearing. This was the stuff of fairy tales. He caught Mariah's eye, and she seemed equally stunned by the idea.

Lady Anne reached for the steps to climb the platform. "The wind will be up soon," she said, "so let's get on with it."

By the time Lady Anne was strapped in the harness, many others from the encampment had lined up along the edge of the drop-off to watch the amazing event. Two men held the wing steady for her as she prepared herself. Lady Elizabeth made a few more tweaks on the harness, then put her hand on her sister's shoulder.

"The Prince is with you," she said soberly.

Lady Anne nodded. She walked to the edge of the platform and hesitated. The ground below fell away fast—too fast for her to survive if the wing didn't work. Rowan felt his heart racing as he considered what this brave young girl was offering to do. He felt Mariah's hand grip his and knew she felt it too.

The moment lingered, and Rowan wondered if perhaps Lady Anne had changed her mind. But suddenly she launched herself into the silent air below. The crowd gasped as the wing plummeted down toward the rocks and dirt. Rowan wanted to turn away as Lady Anne's feet skimmed the hillside. Then she slowly lifted away, gliding like an eagle up from its dive into a valley.

Cheers from a thousand spectators rose as the wing floated effortlessly down the valley off to the northern side of the encampment. They watched with great anticipation as Lady Anne neared the valley floor, wondering if she could stop the glider without disaster. At the last moment it looked as if she shifted her weight. The wing lifted slightly, then gently fell to the ground. The maiden flight of the Eagle Glider, as dubbed by Sir Scott and his brothers and sisters, was a success.

Rowan turned to Sir Fairchild. "Amazing. But why build such a thing?"

Fairchild smiled. "Why indeed?" ▨

FIFTEEN

HIGHER CALLING

That evening, Rowan and Mariah attended the council meeting in one of the large caves at the upper end of the valley. Sir Fairchild was required to sit at the front table with the top thirteen leaders of the Eagle's Nest Resolutes, so Rowan and Mariah stood with Julian. Sir Aldwyn found them and joined them. More than sixty additional leaders attended, including representatives from a dozen other Resolute encampments brought in just for this meeting. Most were Knights of the Prince, but some were not. All were drawn by a sense of loyalty to Cameria and what it represented—a loyalty powerful enough to bring tens of thousands to the mountains in defiance of tyranny.

Rowan felt a similar call to greatness rising in his chest—an exhilaration at being part of something so great and so noble. He would fight for Cameria and its people and win the right to serve the Prince freely once more in this great land.

As the last few men and women entered, he glanced about the room and his eyes landed on a familiar face. The massive knight he had met in Laos leaned against the wall, staring hard at him. It took Rowan a moment to recognize him. He leaned toward Mariah.

"Look," he whispered and nodded toward the man, who looked

almost as if he were guarding the cave's entrance. "It's the knight who saved us at Sir Aldwyn's home."

Mariah turned her head to look, then gazed up at Rowan. "It *is* Sir Lijah. But why is he looking at you like that?"

"I don't know." Rowan fixed his eyes on the leader at the front of the assembly, trying to ignore the steely gaze that seemed to burn into the back of his head.

A white-haired knight stood up to bring the meeting to order. "That is Sir Whitley," Julian whispered.

"Ladies and gentlemen of the Resolutes," Sir Whitley began, his voice echoing powerfully off the walls. "While we slept, our great Cameria fell into the hands of a tyrant, and our freedoms have all but vanished." He allowed the cave to fall silent. "Our swords have been taken, our families imprisoned, our lands procured, our travel restricted, and our businesses taxed to support the very people who want to completely destroy us and our allies. Above all this, as you know, the order of the Knights of the Prince has been banned from Cameria."

At that, the assembly bemoaned their plight with audible disapproval. Sir Whitley held up his hands to regain control of the meeting.

"Though these days are dark, we know that our King and the Prince will be victorious over the evil that is casting its shadow across the kingdom. Cameria can still be a beacon of light that stands against the Dark Knight and his Shadow Warriors!"

This brought a cheer from the assembly, and Rowan felt the passion of the Resolutes reverberate off the walls.

"We have a plan to retake Cameria and restore freedom to the land." Sir Whitley let his words settle into the hearts and minds of his listeners. "Lord Gavaah is powerful, but if we join together and take just one of the five great cities of Cameria, we'll have a base of operations to take the fight to the rest of the region, and we'll show the people of Cameria that we are resolved to fight for freedom. I believe hundreds of thousands will join us if we show them that we are strong and we are united!" Sir Whitley held up a clenched fist to emphasize his point, and the gesture brought thunderous applause.

"Which city?" someone asked.

"Let's take the capital city of Kroywen," another voice called out. "That's where Gavaah is."

Whitley held up his hands again to restore order.

"We considered Kroywen, but that is also where Gavaah's power is concentrated. He commands both the city's sentinels and the armies of the region. No—we shall take Laos, and here is why: Eagle's Nest is the largest Resolute encampment in Cameria, and we are closest to Laos. Additionally, by taking Laos, we will divide Gavaah's forces, isolating Berwick's smaller forces to the south. Retaking Berwick will be much easier without reinforcements from Gavaah. Finally, Laos is nearest the mountains."

"Why is that important?" someone from the back asked.

"Because of this," Whitley said. He reached behind a table and lifted up another model of the glider that Rowan had seen earlier.

"Most of you saw the maiden flight of our Eagle Glider today. Perhaps you wondered why we would spend so much time and energy on such a seemingly fanciful toy. This, my friends"—Whitley held the glider high for all to see—"is how we will conquer Gavaah's forces at Laos and retake the city."

Whitley walked from one side of the assembly to the other. "We only have one chance, fellow knights. Gavaah knows there are Resolutes in the mountains, and he is massing his defenses along the eastern borders of the cities, especially Kroywen. It would be difficult for us to launch a head-on attack against any of these forces and survive. So what we will do is give them what they expect—and also what they don't. We will silently fly thousands of our knights over the top of Gavaah's army, straight into the city, and take control before they have a chance to turn around and fight us. Then, when Gavaah's army turns to fight our knights in the city, we will strike with our regular ground forces from the mountains."

The plan seemed risky and brilliant all at the same time. Many questions and much discussion followed, but in general everyone agreed, and the representatives from the other encampments seemed excited to carry the news back to their people. A date nearly three months hence was set as Freedom Day. There was much work to be done—materials to be gathered, gliders to be built, and both riders and ground fighters to be trained. Everyone in the room seemed eager to be involved.

Almost everyone…

The assembly was dismissed, and the knights began to exit. Rowan had nearly forgotten about Sir Lijah, but when he turned around, he couldn't ignore that hard stare.

"Sir Aldwyn"—Rowan motioned toward the massive knight—"do you know that man?"

"Not really. He's a loner," Aldwyn said. "At first we wondered if perhaps he was a spy for Gavaah, but…"

"He saved us from the sentinels in Laos last summer," Rowan said. "I don't think he would have killed those sentinels if he were a spy."

"Yes, Zetta told me," Aldwyn replied. "She said he was looking for me, but he's never asked me for anything." Aldwyn shook his head. "He won't train or be trained. He won't lead or be led. He asks for nothing except to be allowed to remain with us. In exchange, he hunts for the encampment, and he is very good at it."

"You mean he won't join in the battle for Laos?" Mariah asked.

"He's made it clear that he will not be part of any assault on Gavaah or his forces," Aldwyn said.

"Then he *must* be a spy," Mariah said, quite perturbed. "How can he be a Knight of the Prince and not join this cause?"

"He handled eight sentinels at once," Rowan said to Aldwyn. "His sword would bring much to the fight."

"Perhaps you can talk to him," Aldwyn said.

"I shall," Rowan replied.

When they neared the exit, Rowan deliberately walked toward Sir Lijah.

"I will speak with you," the massive knight said, glaring at Rowan and ignoring everyone else. "Alone," Sir Lijah added when Mariah stepped up beside Rowan.

Rowan looked at Mariah and his friends. "I'll join you in a minute."

Mariah hesitated, then exited the cave with the others.

Rowan crossed his arms and glared back at Sir Lijah. He couldn't help but wonder how he would fare in a duel with the man. The two huge knights silently faced off with such intensity that those around them seemed to feel it. Stragglers quickly sidestepped and left, glancing nervously at the two powerful knights in their stare down.

"Who are you really," Rowan finally asked, "and why are you here?"

Sir Lijah slowly moved his hand to his sword. Rowan felt the tempo of his heart increase. Perhaps this man was more than a spy. Perhaps he was an assassin.

"I'm here for you," Lijah said, slowly drawing his sword.

Rowan stepped back and drew his sword as well.

"What's going on, gentlemen?" Rowan heard Sir Whitley call from behind him. Six or so other men and women voiced exclamations as Rowan faced off with Lijah. Mariah, Julian, and Aldwyn reappeared at the cave entrance.

"Stop!" Mariah shouted, but Rowan didn't dare drop his guard. Everything about this man was more threatening than any he'd ever faced.

"Do something, Julian!" Mariah exclaimed.

"You're kidding, right?" Julian said. He drew his sword, as did Aldwyn, but neither dared step in the way.

"You're not supposed to be here," Lijah muttered through clenched teeth.

Rowan hesitated. *What does that mean?* he wondered.

Lijah engaged with an explosive set of cuts and slices that put Rowan immediately in retreat. Only then did Rowan realize that he'd been tricked by the comment. He countered defensively, trying to adapt quickly to the man's fighting style. Just when he thought he had Lijah figured out, however, a completely new advance would evolve, and Rowan found himself constantly adjusting and retreating.

Their fight moved from one side of the large cave to another, toppling chairs and sending people scurrying out of the way. A few armed men entered the cave, but no one seemed to know what to do. Rowan and Lijah were locked in a duel of such power and intensity there was little anyone could do but watch in amazement.

Other than the mysterious knight long ago that Rowan had come to believe was the Prince, Rowan had never faced such a fighter before. Just when he thought he might lose the fight, he glanced at Mariah and saw the fear in her face. This angered him and renewed his strength. His sword flew faster and stronger until he was able to turn his retreat into an advance against Lijah.

By this time more men had filtered into the cave. Twenty men now stood with swords at ready, but still none dared attempt to stop the fight. Something beyond normal was happening, and many watched with eyes wide and mouths open.

At one point Rowan was late in deflecting a cut, and Lijah's blade sliced his right shoulder. Mariah screamed, but Rowan didn't even feel the wound. He countered so quickly and with such power that his sword blasted back into Lijah's and sliced the knight's left arm. At that, Lijah stopped and held his sword vertically in front of himself.

Rowan recoiled to strike but froze at the last instant. If he executed this cut, Lijah could never recover. It would be the end of him. Both men were sweating profusely and breathing hard. Lijah closed his eyes. The tension in the room hung like a thick cloud. Everyone held their breath, waiting to see how this strange duel would end.

"You don't belong here," Lijah repeated, then opened his eyes and lowered his sword.

"What does that mean?" Rowan panted, still not ready to lower his sword.

Lijah fully relaxed his position and let his sword come to rest on the granite floor. The twenty armed men, including Julian and Aldwyn, quickly came and encircled the two knights.

"I have fought a thousand men looking for you. Your mission is with me, and it is not here."

Rowan slowly lowered his sword, and everyone seemed extremely relieved. Heads turned as Sir Whitley approached the men. "What's the meaning of this?"

Sir Lijah turned to face Sir Whitley. "A friendly contest, sir. My apologies." He gazed blankly at the commander of the Resolutes, and Whitley eyed him in return.

"Take it elsewhere," Whitley said tersely, then turned and left, as did most of the other men. Only Mariah, Aldwyn, and Julian stayed close by.

"Who are you?" Mariah asked Lijah fiercely.

Lijah turned and looked at her directly for the first time. "Rowan and I have a mission together, and I've come for him."

Rowan stared at Lijah, not sure what to think or say but, remarkably, not shocked by the comment. Mariah looked at Rowan for some confirmation or denial, but Rowan could offer neither.

"What mission?" Rowan asked.

"What I have to say is for you and you alone," Lijah said bluntly.

Rowan looked at Aldwyn and Julian, and they backed away but did not leave the cave. Mariah did not move.

"She is my wife," Rowan said to Lijah. "Whatever you tell me, you tell her."

Lijah paused. "Very well."

He stared at Rowan with unreadable eyes. "I was born in Chessington to a common young couple twenty-two years ago. My mother died during the delivery, and the midwife didn't understand why until she realized another child was still in the womb. The midwife was able to save the second child. But my father was greatly distraught by the loss of his wife and succumbed to the plague shortly afterward.

"It was decided that the two infants would be given to separate families, since two newborns would be too much of a burden on any one family. I was raised in the home of a Noble Knight and trained as such, but my new mother secretly believed in the Prince and raised me to believe in Him too. From the time I was a small boy, my mother said that I was destined to proclaim the truth of the Prince in a special way. Later, when I was older, she told me how she knew it was true."

Lijah stopped and glanced from Rowan to Mariah and back again. "One evening she came to my cradle and found a large man holding me.

Before she could call for help, the man walked over to her and placed me in her arms. She said that I was clutching a scroll…this scroll." Lijah reached into his tunic and withdrew a tattered, worn-out parchment. "The man placed a leather strap around my mother's neck—a strap with a key on it. Then he disappeared without saying a single word."

Lijah held the scroll, staring blankly at it. His gaze lifted and pierced Rowan.

"My mother was a noble woman, not given to fanciful imagination. What she said happened is true."

Rowan opened his mouth and then closed it, not knowing what to say. As incredible as the story seemed, he still saw little connection to himself and his life. And yet, strangely, he felt it resonate deep within him. Was it just the strangeness of the story that called to him so?

"What happened to the other child?" Mariah asked.

"The family who adopted that child moved to another region of the kingdom." Lijah stared at Rowan. "To Cameria."

Rowan swallowed hard. Mariah grabbed his arm.

"What are you saying…that I'm your brother?" Rowan asked.

Lijah just kept staring at him.

"Prove it," Rowan finally blurted out.

"I cannot," Lijah replied. "But I need not. You know it to be so."

Rowan couldn't deny that there was something about Lijah that was undeniably and strangely familiar.

"You are not Camerian, Rowan. Your veins flow with the blood of the King's people. We were born in Chessington, descendants of the people of Nan. Though our parents were poor and common, our heritage belongs to the King, His Son, and His people in Chessington…our people."

Rowan turned and walked away a few paces. He had wondered countless times about his origins. Never had he imagined it might be someplace other than Cameria. Could Lijah's story be true?

"Your given name is Mosiah. It means 'to draw out.'" Lijah's voice was low, but loud enough for Rowan to hear. "It is time for you to be drawn out of Cameria."

Rowan turned around and slowly came back. "Why have you come for me now?"

Lijah held out the scroll, but Rowan couldn't make himself take it. If this was all true, what would it mean for him, for Mariah, for the Resolutes?

Mariah reached out and took the scroll from Lijah. She opened it and began to read out loud.

Farewell peace on the river, farewell peace one and all,
Fear not dark in the evening; hear the Prince and His call.
Two babes born in sorrow—a husband weeps for his wife—
One child raised by his people, one child raised in strife,
One marked child with a key, one marked child will roam,
One marked child with an image, one marked child comes home.
The Code, the Key, and the Image, a chamber revealed for two.
A mission beckons My people. Words of the Prince be true.
Two men chosen in armor, abandoning life for the call.
Two men face the Dark One: to Chessington herald…

Mariah looked up from the scroll. "The last two words are unreadable."

Lijah nodded. "My mother said the scroll was torn. She never told me what the last words were."

" 'To Chessington herald…' for all?" Mariah asked, trying to piece together the last few words of the cryptic scroll.

"It's possible," Lijah said.

Lijah pulled a leather cord from around his neck and held a tarnished key in his hand.

Mariah studied the parchment again. "If you were the child with the key, and you really are brothers, that would mean Rowan was the child with the image. What image?"

Lijah shrugged. "Were you given an image of something as a child?"

Rowan shook his head.

"A pendant, medallion, birthmark…anything?" Lijah pressed.

"No…nothing." Rowan felt himself becoming agitated. The words on the scroll could mean anything. He shook his head and turned away again.

"You must come with me, Mosiah," Lijah said, "to Chessington."

Rowan's nostrils flared. He turned back and pointed at Lijah. "No! My name is Rowan. Can't you see what's happening here? We are preparing for battle against Gavaah and his army. How do you know our mission isn't right here, right now?"

"Don't you understand?" Lijah returned fiercely. "This isn't about Laos. This isn't even about Cameria. This is about Chessington. The days are short. The Dark Knight is rising in power, and the coming of the Prince is near. Our calling is higher than this. We have a mission that awaits us elsewhere in Arrethtrae."

Rowan froze, captured by the familiar words. And yet Lijah's story, the scroll, the key—it all seemed so strange. Frustration rose up in him as he struggled to take it all in.

Lijah stepped toward Rowan. "I don't know why we were chosen or even what we were chosen for. I just know it has to do with Chessington—and soon!"

Rowan studied Lijah through narrowed eyes. "If this is all true, how did you know to find me here? You were here even before I was. How is that possible?"

The fierceness of Lijah's countenance diminished, and he seemed hesitant to answer. He looked to the ground as if he didn't want to.

"I began looking for you more than four years ago—first in Chessington, then in the Outdweller regions. A year and half ago is when I finally learned that you had been taken to Cameria, but still that was not enough. Ten months ago, just before I first saw you at Laos, I had a very vivid dream… At least, I think it was a dream. In the dream, the Prince told me that if I found the man named Aldwyn, I would find my brother."

Lijah looked up at Rowan. "And so I have, for there is not another in all the kingdom who fights like we do. We were born to use the sword, Mosiah. At least tell me you know that much to be true."

Rowan stared at Lijah, pondering the strange knight's call, then finally shook his head. "I will fight with my people here in Cameria," he said. "They need me, and they need you. Come, Mariah." He held out his hand for her to take, and together they walked to the entrance of the cave.

Later that night, Mariah rubbed Rowan's brow to soothe him, but she was as silent as he.

"You are troubled, my wife, as I am." Rowan looked up into her beautiful eyes. "You needn't worry. I'll not leave you."

Mariah forced a smile, but he could tell she was still disturbed.

Rowan sat up and gently took her hands. "What is it, darling?"

Mariah looking lovingly and deeply into his eyes. "You *do* have an image."

Sixteen

THE BATTLE FOR LAOS

 "An image… What do you mean?" Rowan asked. "Where? Where is the image?"

"It's on your back, on your right shoulder," Mariah said sadly. "I first saw it after I freed you from the cave, when I was helping you change your tunic. It's…unique."

Rowan's heart began to pound. "What does it look like?"

"Lift your shirt," she said.

She took a pen and a parchment and carefully copied the mark. When she was done, she gave it to Rowan.

The shape looked like a sun with varying lengths and widths of sunbeams shining forth from it. He stared at it for a long time, then finally looked at Mariah.

She bit her lip. "What does this mean?"

"It means I have a strange-looking birthmark and nothing is going to change." He pulled her to him. "I'm not leaving you, Mariah. My duty is here, with you…with our people. We will raise our children in a free Cameria. All right?"

Mariah nodded and sank into his embrace.

As the days passed, however, he often saw her lost in thought.

♛ ♛ ♛

The next three months flew by in a frenzy of activity as war preparations and training escalated and all activity in Eagle's Nest focused on Freedom Day. Rowan volunteered to fly one of the gliders into the city, and his time was soon consumed with training for flight.

Building the gliders had proved to be the most resource-consuming task of all the preparations, for they had to be collapsible for the trek around to the west side of the mountain and then capable of being quickly and securely erected for flight. Sir Scott and his team were constantly making modifications to the gliders as well as training the fliers. Soon the air above the valley was constantly filled with gliders and riders.

The drawback to such an attack was that those who flew the gliders could not wear heavy armor. Modified leather armor would have to do, and it was hoped that the advantage of the surprise attack would offset their armor disadvantage.

Even with lighter armor, Rowan's glider required additional wingspan and structural support for his large, muscular frame. The trainers were nervous about his first training flight, as was he. The first few seconds of drastic drop left him breathless, but as the glider caught the air and lifted him up, he yelled with excitement. It was the most freeing sensation he'd ever experienced. He quickly learned to control his flight path by leaning and shifting his weight.

He had been told that landing would be a bit more challenging, especially because of his weight, and that certainly proved to be true. He twisted an ankle and tore his leather armor on the first attempt. After two more flights, however, his landings became smooth, even those designed to simulate landing in the close quarters of city streets.

The simultaneous ground assault was to be executed by the other encampments, since they didn't have access to the gliders or the training. Resolutes from those encampments began arriving two weeks prior to Freedom Day, carefully positioning themselves in the forest of the mountain's western face.

Through it all, Lijah kept his distance from Rowan. For most of the daylight hours, the large knight hunted, providing meat for the Eagle's Nest encampment. In the evenings, Rowan often saw him perched on a large boulder overlooking the encampment. Rowan tried to ignore the apparent coincidences of Lijah's story, but every night his mind filled with questions that seemed impossible to answer. He was thankful for Mariah, and their love for each other grew stronger as Freedom Day approached.

They had decided that she would help with the launches of the gliders and then remain on the mountain until the battle was over. This decision gave Rowan great peace, but Mariah seemed to grow more anxious with each passing day.

The last two weeks of preparation seemed endless and impossible, but on the eve of the battle for Laos, all was ready. Tomorrow they would travel to the opposite side of the mountain and prepare for launch at first light of the following morning. Whitley received word that the ground forces were in place. Freedom Day was here.

Rowan and Mariah walked back from the briefing in the upper cave, discussing what they had heard from the leaders. Rowan sensed the anticipation, the hope, and the anxiety of the Resolutes. Two men had just returned from Thecia with a report that the strongman of Chessington, Alexander Histen, had now gained control over half the kingdom, and it seemed no one could stop him. This was oppressive news for the people of Eagle's Nest. It meant that even if they were victorious tomorrow, the victory would only be the beginning of a long war to freedom.

Rowan glanced up at the boulder and saw Lijah there, watching as he had been for the last three months. Rowan stopped, and Mariah held tightly to his arm.

"I must talk to him one more time," Rowan said.

"I know," Mariah replied. She kissed Rowan and then released him.

Rowan climbed up the boulder and stood face to face with Lijah.

"How can you see what is happening here and just stand by and do nothing?" Rowan asked. "These people need you."

"The future of these people is not determined by what happens here but by what happens in Chessington." Lijah crossed his arms. "You are jeopardizing that future by participating in a battle that is not yours to fight." Lijah took a deep breath, flaring his nostrils on the exhale. "If you should die tomorrow, our mission for the Prince will never happen, and the Dark Knight will win."

"You don't know that, Lijah. That is only what you think will happen. I will not abandon these people and my wife based on some bizarre story you may have dreamed up." Rowan shook his head. "My mission is here with my Camerian brothers and sisters. I stand and fight with them. For whom do you fight?"

Lijah glared at Rowan. "I fight for the King…and His Son!"

Rowan glared back. "So do I. And when the battle is over—win or lose, live or die—I will know I have upheld the Code and did not abandon a fellow knight in battle or in peril."

Rowan turned around and left without another word. It was a bitter parting, and Rowan vowed that his parting with Mariah would not be so.

The next morning, more than eleven thousand people began their trek to the western face of the mountain. Nearly eight thousand glider riders made the journey with their crafts, with three thousand supporters to help carry gear and prepare the launches. A surveying team had previously calculated a hundred favorable launch sites for the riders, but even so, launching all eight thousand gliders would require just over two hours.

By sundown, all was ready. The force camped quietly, without fires to give themselves away, trying to sleep but mostly wide-eyed with anticipation.

The first glow of the morning sun initiated Freedom Day, and the gliders began to launch. They had hoped for a still morning, and the winds seemed to comply. The glowing lamps of the city stretched out far before and below them. Soon the sky was filled with thousands of gliders and their riders, skimming trees and mountaintops, on their way to the waking city of Laos. It was an eerie and glorious sight.

Rowan was to lead twenty special riders who would maneuver as close to the city consulate as possible, overcome the security sentinels, and capture Prefect Corsan, who ruled the city. Rowan and his unit were the best swordsmen of the camp, assigned to the most important mission of the battle. Their launch position was higher, for their flight was the longest. Their launch time was planned for thirty minutes after the initial wave, and the time was now.

Mariah kissed him once more before stepping aside, her eyes shining with unshed tears. "The Prince be with you!"

"And with you, my lovely Mariah."

"Come back to me, Rowan," she whispered.

"I will," he said. Then he set his eyes toward Laos and launched.

The first step took his breath away as the ground dropped out from below him. This was quite different from the training flights. Within just a few moments, he was thousands of feet above the ground, looking down on what looked like the whole kingdom.

The skies filled with more gliders, and Rowan felt the thrill of battle coursing through his veins. The cool morning air whistled past his helmet and chilled his gloved hands.

The scene was silently surreal. This flight would last longer than any of the training flights at Eagle's Nest—much longer. Though the shadow of the mountains still obscured much of the city, Rowan began to make out Gavaah's forces in a semicircular formation around the eastern perimeter. Still high in the sky, the force of airborne riders was apparently as yet undetected, for there were no shouts of alarm.

With each moment that passed, hundreds more gliders launched. Rowan looked behind himself and felt chills run up and down his spine as he saw six thousand more gliders soaring like eagles to fall upon their prey. The kingdom of Arrethtrae had never before been witness to such a bold and daring assault against the evil of tyranny.

Rowan looked right and left and began to see the gliders separate into formations based on their assigned targets. His advance team was identified by the painted blue tips of each triangular wing. Rowan counted only eighteen of the assigned twenty soaring around him. It would have to do.

He pinpointed the consulate building and made a slight adjustment in his flight path. The rest of the team aligned themselves in a wedge formation behind and above him.

There was something majestic about the opening scene of this battle. It wasn't just for Laos they were fighting, or even Cameria. This was a stand against tyranny in every region of the kingdom. What happened this day would resonate and echo through hundreds of castles and cities throughout the land.

Rowan saw the first gliders land below him, followed quickly by shouts of alarm and the clash of swords. The battle was underway. He chanced one last look behind him at the city's perimeter, where the defensive forces were massed. He saw movement back toward the city as thousands of gliders began to land behind them; then the shouts of ten thousand knights rose up as the ground assault from the foothills began.

Rowan focused back on their target, just moments away. Sir Scott's calculations had been nearly spot-on. They would land just two buildings shy of the consulate. Those who were awake below them looked up with mouths hanging open as the airborne force of Resolutes descended into the streets. A contingent of ten mounted sentinels began shouting alarms, and soon mounted sentinels were making their way down the street toward them.

Rowan was the first of his unit to land. He drew his dagger and sliced through the harness in an instant, freeing himself from the glider. One sentinel was nearly on him. Rowan drew his sword and sliced through the advancing steed's chest, toppling both horse and sentinel. One of Rowan's team, who had just landed, finished the job with a quick thrust, and the rest of the team sprang to action as they landed one by one.

Soon all eighteen of Rowan's unit were advancing toward the consulate. Resistance was yet minimal; evidently, their surprise had been successful. They approached the steps of the consulate knowing that once they gained entrance, finding Prefect Corsan would be paramount. Five more sentinels rushed upon them from the entrance, but Rowan's team made quick work of them. Now Rowan could hear the roar of battle throughout the entire eastern half of Laos. To Rowan it was the sound of freedom.

Rowan led the charge into the consulate, systematically clearing the building of the enemy. Rowan assigned sentries at access points on the first floor, then led the remaining ten knights to the second floor. Six more sentinels went down, and Rowan lost one man in the skirmish. At last they reached the door to the prefect's chamber. Rowan blasted through it and into Prefect Corsan's chamber, with three other knights on his heels.

A man stood up from his chair, his face white with fear. Rowan held his sword to the man's chest.

"You are under arrest for treason against the people of Cameria," Rowan proclaimed.

"It's not him." The knight next to Rowan lowered his sword. "It's not Corsan."

Rowan advanced, and the man backed up until he was cowering in the corner.

"Where is Corsan?" Rowan demanded.

The man stammered nothing coherent.

"Where?" Rowan shouted.

"He…he fled the city," was all the man could say, but it was enough. Rowan's eyes suddenly grew wide as realization dawned.

"Out!" Rowan yelled. He ran to the door. "Everyone out!" He and his unit retreated down to the main floor and ran into the street to discover a horror waiting for them.

One hundred sentinels immediately surrounded them, swords at ready, while thousands more marched past them from the west toward the battle in the east. Sitting smugly atop a powerful black steed was a man Rowan recognized but who looked nothing like the man he had known. Gone was the fanciful facade of tournament organizer. Lord Gavaah now looked every bit what he was—a powerful Shadow Warrior.

Rowan's men looked to him for some sign of what to do, but there was no choice. To fight against this force would be suicide.

"Well, well, well." Gavaah's distinctive voice carried easily over the sounds of marching feet. "The long-lost Sir Rowan returns as a rebel." Gavaah laughed. "Once again you've played the part of a fool!"

Rowan's jaw tightened, and he clenched the hilt of his sword, but he did not move. All around him the sound of clashing swords and the screams of dying men stained the air.

"It's over, Rowan," Gavaah exclaimed. "What you hear is the complete and total destruction of the Resolute army. Twenty thousand of my men are descending on the Resolutes as we speak. Die with them if you want. It matters not to me."

Rowan thought of Mariah and the families of his comrades. He was not afraid to die, and he knew they weren't either, but it was foolish to die a meaningless death. It took more strength for him to release his grip on his sword than it would have to wield it against these defenders of tyranny, but he did so to save the lives of his unit. There would be another day to fight if he kept their hearts beating.

He dropped his sword, and the other seventeen men did the same. The sentinels fell upon them.

Gavaah urged his horse close to Rowan and looked down on him with utter arrogance.

"How did you know?" Rowan asked as his hands were bound behind him.

Gavaah smiled. "I didn't. I guessed—although you knaves aren't so hard to figure out. Kroywen was too obvious. Laos was closest to the mountains and your miserable encampments." Gavaah looked to the gliders, now broken and strewn about the city street, and sighed deeply. "I suppose some credit must be given for the attack from the air. That was quite remarkable. Pointless, but remarkable…"

Gavaah caught himself and sneered down at Rowan. "Take them to the prisons. If any resist, kill them immediately!"

Rowan wanted to cover his ears to keep from hearing the death cry of freedom in Cameria…and perhaps in Arrethtrae. Was this truly the end of liberty for the people?

How could this be? he asked. *Through Gavaah, the Dark Knight had conquered Cameria… How could this be?*

More important, what would it mean for the entire kingdom?

SEVENTEEN

THE CONQUEST
OF CAMERIA

Rowan and a handful of other prisoners who had been identified as leaders of the Resolutes were taken to Kroywen and imprisoned there. He searched for Julian among the prisoners but could not find him. He was grateful that Mariah was safe in the mountains with her father and Sir Aldwyn, but he knew she'd be sick with worry once she'd received news of the Resolutes' defeat.

After three weeks in the Kroywen prison, Rowan was taken to Lord Gavaah. Two large warriors stood guard behind Rowan to his left and right, and his hands were bound behind him. Yet he thought that Gavaah appeared much more amicable toward him than when he'd last seen him in Laos.

"Rowan, I understand that your journey these past two years has been rather, ah, challenging." Lord Gavaah stood from his chair and adjusted his cape—or was it a robe? Rowan couldn't tell. In fact, Lord Gavaah's chamber, seat, and attire felt more like a throne room than anything else.

Gavaah took a few commanding strides to reach Rowan. "It is fortuitous that you were not killed in that little skirmish in Laos"—he crossed his arms and smiled—"both for you and for me."

Rowan remembered back to when he received his victory cloak

from Gavaah and how struck he had been by the man's grandiose personality. Now, the more he was in the man's presence, the more disgusted he was by Gavaah.

"Now that the rebels have been completely destroyed," Gavaah said, "I have forged a New Cameria—and a new alliance with Governor Supreme Alexander Histen of Chessington. He will soon be ruler of Arrethtrae, and I will rule along with him." Gavaah brushed some lint from his cape as if to emphasize the ease with which he had defeated the Resolutes. He cleared his throat. "There is a place for you here, Rowan. You were perhaps the greatest tournament fighter I have ever seen, and I want to offer you a chance to reclaim that which is rightfully yours."

Rowan couldn't believe what he was hearing. "Your New Cameria is an enslaved Cameria," he said, "and my tournament days are over."

Gavaah laughed. "Oh, I hardly think so. Think of it—you fight for me once again, and I will make you the champion of New Cameria. You will have great wealth, fame, and even power if you want it." Gavaah leaned closer, and his smooth voice sharpened to a sadistic edge. "And what's left for you if you don't? I can have you killed or just leave you to rot in prison until you are nothing but an emaciated worm."

Rowan swallowed hard as he remembered those horrific days in the cave. Gavaah's tempting words licked at him like a serpent hypnotizing its prey, and for one brief moment, he considered Gavaah's offer. How bad would it be to accept this life rather than a life of imprisonment? This mission was a failure anyway. The cause was clearly lost. Perhaps this way he could even use his wealth and influence to reunite with Mariah and actually help the Knights of the Prince?

Gavaah waited, his dark eyes gleaming, clearly enjoying Rowan's discomfort.

Rowan hung his head in discouragement and confusion. Then the words of the Prince whispered once more in his heart: *You are a mighty knight of the King. Time is short, and I have a mission that awaits you.*

Rowan straightened, jarred from his momentary weakness. This was a defining moment in his life, and suddenly he understood it. He was still alive, and the Prince still wanted to use him somehow. He couldn't understand how it could be possible, but still he chose to believe.

"No, Gavaah," he said. "I will not fight for you. Your tournaments weakened the people, allowing you to conquer them, and I will have no part of that." He looked straight into Gavaah's hard stare. "I live for the Prince, and I will fight for Him and Him alone!"

Gavaah glared at Rowan, his smile slowly transforming into a sadistic sneer. The moment lasted a long time.

"How unfortunate you have chosen such a path for yourself." Gavaah turned and walked away, talking as he went. "My Bread and Tournaments strategy was brilliant, I must say, for it captured the time and money of Camerians everywhere. But best of all, it captured their passion and put them to sleep."

Gavaah spun about with a triumphant grin on his face. "Why, I have even seen Followers ten times more passionate about my tournaments—and the knights who fought in them—than they ever were for your pathetic Prince.

"And you helped me do it!" Gavaah's laughter swelled as he pointed an accusing finger. Rowan cringed, for he knew it was true.

"But you were too good, Rowan. I could see that controlling your popularity—and thus controlling you—would prove to be difficult, especially before I had complete control of the land."

Rowan's eyes widened as he realized what Gavaah was saying.

"Surprised? Really, Rowan, do you think anything about life is fair? You were supposed to die, but those imbeciles thought they knew better."

Gavaah looked away and sighed. "But fortunately all has worked out for the better. You see, when a dog kills and tastes blood for the first time, it will always—*always*—want more."

A grim smile formed on Gavaah's thin lips as he came and stood close to Rowan again. "And that's exactly what the people of New Cameria want."

Gavaah let loose an evil chortle that made Rowan shudder. The dark soul of this man was becoming more evident with each word he spoke.

"My games are no longer Bread and Tournaments," he said. "Now they are Blood and Tournaments. The people love it, and their insatiable desire for more is exhilarating!" Gavaah raised both arms in the air.

"The people of Cameria have been tricked and lied to by you, Gavaah." Rowan spoke to cut Gavaah's self-worship short. "I believe they are still good people. You haven't destroyed their hearts…not yet. When they hear the truth, they will realize who you are and what you've done."

"What a fool you are." Gavaah put a hand before him and slowly closed it into a fist. "I own them all!" Gavaah leaned in closely to Rowan. "You will fight for me, Rowan, or you will die."

Rowan raised his chin in defiance. "Then I will die."

Gavaah smiled. "So be it. You see, my ignorant, naive little knight, the people want to be fed and entertained, so I give them bread and entertain them. In exchange, they give me the power to rule over them. It's a wonderful exchange. In the meantime, Master Lucius can once again focus on the conquest of Chessington without the hindrance of aid from Cameria."

Gavaah's statement jolted Rowan. It was just as Lijah and Sir Aldwyn had said. It truly was all about Chessington. Had he made a mistake in staying with the Resolutes instead of following Lijah?

Gavaah was not through. "You Arrethtraens are so simpleminded. In spite of your little raid on one of my cities, I have done my job well, and *you* have helped me. You see, I didn't need an army to conquer Cameria. Not at first. I just needed a few skilled, arrogant knights. Cameria now belongs to me, and there is nothing you can do to change it!"

In this dark hour, Rowan finally understood what was happening. Everything came back to the ultimate battle between the Prince and Lucius, even the manipulation of his life by Gavaah. He felt like a pawn that had been played and trapped by his own pride, then sacrificed without a thought. Anger and humiliation burned in his bosom.

"Good, Rowan. I see the anger burning in your eyes. You will need it when you fight for me."

"Though it cost me my life," Rowan said through clenched teeth, "I will never fight for you!"

Gavaah slowly walked behind Rowan. "You *will* fight for me at least once," he whispered, "and it will be the greatest game Cameria has ever seen!"

He motioned with a flourish that set his coat swirling. "Guards, take him away."

Rowan spent the next two weeks in the city prison, isolated from the other prisoners. Though carefully guarded, he was left free of chains, fed well, and even allowed a daily walk in the sunshine. This special treatment made him very suspicious of Gavaah's future plan for him. Rowan resolved in his heart to be wary and watch for any opportunity of escape that might present itself. In the meantime, he was willing to wait and be ready for whatever the Prince required of him next—even if it meant sacrificing his life.

On the morning of a brilliant blue day, Rowan was transferred from the prison to the Kroywen stadium. He tried not to marvel at the elaborate and opulent structure, but couldn't help it. Gavaah had built a temple of entertainment worship that was extravagant in the extreme, and he obviously still expected Rowan to partake in the spectacle.

The sounds of tens of thousands of spectators began to rumble down into the lower chambers where knights and combatants prepared for battle. There were numerous lesser duels and even some simulated battles prior to the fight that Gavaah expected Rowan to fight in. Evidently Rowan's fight would be the climactic duel of the day.

They're going to be extremely disappointed, Rowan thought.

He looked up at the ceiling above him. He could hear and feel the cheering, chanting, and stomping in a stadium that could hold fifty thousand spectators. Just a few short years ago, he would have given anything for a chance to fight in front of such a crowd. Now he simply wondered what would happen when he refused the battle.

Servants arrived to strip Rowan of his clothes and then began strapping on scant leather armor that made him look more like a marauder than a knight. When he protested, sentinels drew their swords and forced him to be still. It was just as he had heard. The days of fighting for honor were a thing of the past, and the elite professional knights had been replaced by cutthroat combatants.

By the time they were through with him, Rowan's muscular body glistened with sweat, for the heat of the lower chambers was significant. Above him, the crowd seemed to be in a near frenzy.

The servants placed Rowan on an elaborate horse-drawn cart and locked his wrists to the side rails with iron bindings. He felt like a living trophy for Gavaah to parade in front of the people.

A driver took the reins of the team of horses and waited. As the gates opened, the sound of the cheering crowd swelled to a deafening roar. Slowly the noise of the crowd abated until one lone voice could be heard—Lord Gavaah's familiar ringing baritone.

"People of Cameria," Gavaah's practiced voice echoed across the stadium. "Today I bring to you a great contest beyond anything you have yet seen!"

A great cheer arose, then diminished to allow Gavaah to continue.

"I have captured one of the leaders of the fanatical rebels who attempted an assault on our great city of Laos, where thousands of innocent citizens died. Our laws require him to be sentenced to death for his grievous crimes against the people of Cameria. Out of mercy, I have given him a chance to die honorably in a fight rather than to hang shamelessly from a noose.

"Is this not justice?" Gavaah's voice rose in volume. "Is this not mercy?" He shouted passionately to stir the people, and they responded in kind. The stadium shook with roaring shouts of acclamation. Rowan was sickened not only by Gavaah's twisted mind and silver tongue but by the frenzied crowd. How could the people be led so easily? Was it the thrill and energy of the stadium arena that inspired their gullibility? Rowan concluded that it was. He was astounded by the force of a crowd over the minds of individuals.

After waiting for the cheers of the crowd to build, the driver slapped the reins, and the cart lurched forward. Rowan widened his stance to keep his balance as they entered the arena. The crowd reached an entirely new level of riotous roaring as Rowan emerged into their view. He looked full circle around him, awed in spite of himself at the spectacle.

The stadium was filled with people from all walks of life. Gavaah and his cronies sat beneath a canopied grandstand, surrounded by sentinels and warriors. Seated on each side of the grandstand were men and women of Arrethtraen nobility and elevated stature. Each subsequent section diminished in social stature until the remaining majority of the seats were filled with many thousands of commoners.

The cart and its trophy first traveled slowly in front of the elite grandstand. Rowan locked eyes with Gavaah as he passed, enduring the tyrant's condescending glare. The cart then began to travel around the perimeter of the arena, and the crowd's cheers turned to angry taunting. As Rowan absorbed the glares and jeers of thousands of angry people, his heart became heavy, for Gavaah's description of the people and their insatiable appetite for violent entertainment seemed gruesomely accurate. *Has Cameria completely lost its heart for that which is good?* he wondered sadly.

Rowan looked up defiantly into the taunting crowd. Then something strange began to happen. One man stopped shouting and pointed at him with a face of recognition. Rowan saw him turn to the man next to him and mouth his name. The people in that section became silent as they realized that this prisoner was the mighty Sir Rowan of Laos.

As the cart continued its circuit around the stadium, the noise of the crowd subsided, giving way to an eerie silence. When the cart passed once more in front of Lord Gavaah, a quiet but steadily growing cheer rose up from the commoners, starting on the far side of the stadium.

"Rowan! Rowan! Rowan!"

Soon the entire stadium shook with the rhythmic sound of Rowan's name being shouted by thousands. Rowan looked up at Gavaah and saw frustration and anger. This, clearly, was unexpected.

Gavaah held out his arms to gain control of the crowd, but they resisted. Finally, after numerous attempts to quell them and speak, Gavaah gained the crowd's attention.

"People of Cameria!" Gavaah shouted. "The name and reputation of a man does not free him from the law. Sir Rowan of Laos is guilty of treason and must pay for his crimes against our great region!"

Many in the elite areas began to clap, but jeers and boos rose up from the commoners. Gavaah tried to recover the people again but could not. His anger turned to fury, and Rowan gained no small amount of satisfaction in seeing Gavaah nearly beside himself.

The jeers of the crowd turned once more to a chant for Rowan, and this seemed to put Gavaah over the edge. He gathered his warriors around him and walked down the grandstand steps into the arena. He stared up at Rowan, fury burning in his eyes. Then he jumped onto the cart and stood with his face just inches from Rowan's. Rowan would have given anything for one free hand, but the bindings held him tight.

"Enjoy this while you can, Rowan." Gavaah looked about at the cheering people. "Whether you win or lose, I will have my fight *and* my execution today."

"I will not give you the satisfaction of a fight, Gavaah," Rowan said calmly.

Gavaah's countenance contorted into an evil smile. "You *will* fight, Rowan, because I know something you and they"—he motioned toward the chanting crowd—"don't know."

Gavaah signaled, and a set of gates opened. Another cart entered the stadium with another knight strapped to its rails. This knight, however, was arrayed in full armor with helmet and visor in place. The cart came near and halted.

"You see, it wasn't very difficult to locate the rest of the rebels once we saw the gliders." Gavaah let his words soak into Rowan's mind, and his heart skipped a beat as he considered what Gavaah was saying. Gavaah nodded to one of the guards, who jumped up into the other cart, grabbed the helmet of the knight, and lifted the visor for Rowan to see.

He could only see her eyes, but it was enough. There beneath the armor was his beautiful Mariah. Her eyes were filled with fear. Rowan felt as if a knife had pierced his heart.

"Rowan!" Mariah cried out, but the warrior quickly snapped the visor back in place and jumped from the cart.

"Mariah!" Rowan screamed, but the name was lost in the chant of the crowd. He pulled against the iron bindings.

Gavaah signaled again, and the driver of Mariah's cart bolted away toward the center of the arena. Once there, the driver unharnessed the horse from the cart and led the animal away, leaving Mariah and the cart behind. All the while the crowd continued to chant, unknowingly immersing Rowan and Mariah in a death chant that happened to be his own name.

Out of the open gate, six large men dressed similar to Rowan entered the stadium and walked to stand between Rowan and Mariah, a distance of about fifty paces.

Rowan clenched his teeth and pulled frantically against his bonds. "Let her go, Gavaah!" Rowan demanded. Then he sagged in defeat. "Let her go...and I will fight for you."

"Oh, it's much too late for that, Rowan," Gavaah said. "I've devised something far more entertaining than a mere fight between you and other knights. Look at these warriors, Rowan." Gavaah gestured as if he were explaining the simple rules of a game to someone. "The combatant who kills you receives a weighty sum of gold. The combatant who kills the other knight, your lovely wife, will receive the same amount if and only if you are killed first. If, however, you prove too difficult to kill, any one of them can decide to kill her and receive half the gold—not nearly as rewarding, but a much easier prize."

Gavaah looked toward Mariah. "You and I are the only ones here that know who she is. That makes the fight so much more enjoyable, don't you agree? Oh, and for every combatant you defeat, another will join from the gate...and another...and another...until both of you are dead." He gave a wicked chuckle. "It's quite remarkable what men will do for a little gold."

Gavaah looked around and seemed to now enjoy the chanting he heard. "They don't know it yet, but they will love this day and the blood I bring them...and they will want more. It is the way of the human heart, Rowan."

Gavaah looked deep into Rowan's eyes and sneered. "Good-bye, my stupid Arrethtraen knight."

The driver of Rowan's cart had released the horse's harness and led the animal back into the gate while they were talking. Now Gavaah and his guards moved to their seats in the grandstand, and the driver returned. He set a sword in the ground, then climbed into the cart with a key to unlock the shackles binding Rowan's wrists. The man's hands were shaking so badly he could hardly fit the key into the lock.

"Hurry up, man!" Rowan looked anxiously at Mariah and the six combatants who stood between him and his love.

Finally the man found the opening to the lock and turned the key. As soon as his right hand was free, Rowan grabbed the key from the man and pushed him out of the way. He quickly opened the other lock and jumped down to grab the sword. He looked beyond the combatants to his still-shackled wife and dared not think about the odds. He must play Gavaah's twisted execution game even if there was no hope of winning.

"Rowan! Rowan! Rowan!" the crowd continued to chant, not knowing just how cruel this day could become.

EIGHTEEN

A HOPELESS FIGHT

Rowan had to get to Mariah quickly before any of the combatants became impatient with the fight. He approached the men, and the largest of them was the first to engage. Three others positioned themselves to Rowan's right and left, while the remaining two began to circle behind him. Rowan quickly disengaged to drop the weaker of the two. As he reached to recover the man's weapon so he could fight with two swords, another combatant entered the arena from the gate behind them.

After two more engagements and one more fatal wound to one of the combatants, Rowan's mastery was obvious, despite the odds. The ferocity with which he executed his moves bought him the hesitancy he needed from his opponents. They knew that if they came within reach of either of Rowan's swords, they would die or be seriously wounded.

The crowd did indeed love the fight and cheered all the more for Rowan. Rowan tried time and time again to maneuver toward Mariah, and though he was able to close the distance, his opponents maintained their positions between them. He dared not draw any closer, for close proximity would also decrease the time he had to react if one of the combatants decided to take his sword to her instead.

Keeping track of all six men was at first more than Rowan thought he could do, but soon his mind and body had elevated to a whole new level of functioning. It seemed impossible that any of the combatants could penetrate his defenses with a sword. All they could do was hope to wear him down.

Three more encounters left another combatant incapacitated, but he too was quickly replaced. Rowan saw one of the original six combatants turn and look at Mariah, and he knew the time was short. The desperation of the scene forced him to adapt to a whole new fight. His mind and sword worked in perfect sync—analyzing, slicing, projecting, cutting, decoying, and thrusting.

Rowan fought with two and three men at a time, engaging each only long enough to keep the others from advancing. With each mistake a combatant made, a body fell to the ground. Rowan saw the man who had earlier looked at Mariah drop his sword ever so slightly, and he knew he must act now if he was going to save her life. The man's foot shifted, and Rowan intensified his assault against the two men he was currently fighting. After three quick cuts, both opponents went down, but the delay gave the retreating man time to break away.

"No!" Rowan abandoned all caution in pursuit of the man. When he felt the tip of another combatant's blade slice across his back, he planted his foot, spun about, cut through the man, and continued on, hardly missing a step.

The leading combatant was now almost to Mariah, who tugged hopelessly against her bindings. The crowd roared in both excitement and fear as the fight hurtled toward a gruesome end. Rowan wished desperately that time would stop, for he was simply too far behind the man to reach her before the combatant did.

Suddenly a commotion arose from the right side of the stadium. A large figure draped in a black cloak jumped from the commoners' stands and began running toward Mariah. The crowd roared its approval as the man drew a gleaming sword from his belt.

Rowan dared not even stop to glance at the newcomer or hope that he had come to help. Perhaps some citizen wanted the gold too.

Now eight men were racing toward Mariah and the cart that held her in the center of the arena, but only one would be first. The combatant was nearly there, and Rowan watched in agony as the man mounted the cart. The next closest was the man wearing the cloak, but he was still ten paces away and would be too late as well, no matter what his intentions were.

The combatant drew back his blade. Mariah pulled back from him, pulling desperately against her restraints, as Rowan screamed her name.

Suddenly the man in black stopped running, threw off his cloak, and drew a short sword. Rowan was stunned to see Sir Lijah take aim and let the weapon fly toward Mariah's executioner. The brute's blade began its plunge toward her heart, and Rowan faltered, but just before the tip of the brute's blade touched Mariah's breastplate, Lijah's sword sunk solidly into the man's torso, and he collapsed against the side rail.

Lijah took up a defensive position for Lady Mariah as Rowan took his sword and hacked through the wooden side rails that held her iron bindings. Mariah then recovered the fallen combatant's sword and joined Rowan and Lijah against the remaining combatants.

Gavaah rose to his feet, infuriated by the interruption of his execution, and ordered all remaining combatants into the arena. More than twenty armed men rushed upon Rowan, Lijah, and Mariah from two different gates. The crowd gasped at the impending bloodbath, then resumed cheering.

The fight seemed to rage on endlessly. Fourteen combatants fell before Lijah took a cut across his left shoulder. Rowan moved to cover him, but both men were tiring and began to make mistakes. Mariah fought gallantly, but when Rowan took a cut to his thigh, he recoiled, leaving her exposed for a moment too long. She deflected a cut from one combatant, but a second plunged his sword through her breastplate and into her chest.

"Mariah!" Rowan felt his soul crumble as she fell to the ground. With one powerful blow, he cut her attacker down in an instant. More combatants fell to Lijah's sword as he rallied to defend Mariah. Only four combatants now remained, but Rowan didn't care. He dropped his sword and fell beside his wife. Lijah covered them both, taking two more combatants down. The last two hesitated, then slowly backed away.

All the stadium hushed to hear the wails of the mighty Sir Rowan. He gently took her helmet off and cradled her in his arms.

She looked up at him, struggling with the pain, and tried to smile. "My...love," she whispered.

Rowan's eyes swam with tears.

He shook his head. "No, Mariah. Please stay with me. I can't live without you!"

Mariah shook her head. "You...must live. The Prince...calls you."

Rowan's tears spilled onto her cheeks. She coughed and squeezed her eyes shut, wheezing in pain. When she opened her eyes, she lifted a gentle hand to Rowan's cheek.

He covered her hand with his own and leaned to within an inch of her face. "Please...," he whispered. "No...."

"You...you're the one the scroll speaks of." Her voice was faint. "Always knew there was something...special about you."

Mariah winced, and Rowan tried to shush her, but she shook her head. "Your destiny...the call of the King." She managed to smile at him. "My love..."

Her hand slowly fell away from his face as she slumped in his arms. He gathered her close and screamed against the crushing ache in his bosom. All the kingdom seemed to fall silent as Rowan wept bitterly for his bride.

Then, gradually, the pain within him hardened to a slow-burning anger—against Gavaah, his warriors, the combatants, and the people's lust for violent entertainment.

Rowan lifted his head and looked about the stadium with tears streaming down his face. He lifted Mariah in his arms and held her out to the thousands who had watched his love die.

"Is this what you want?" he shouted to them all. He lifted her higher. "Is this what you came here to see? The execution of my wife? The murder of an innocent woman?"

Rowan turned around full circle for all to see the culmination of their lust for the games. "Is this truly what Gavaah has turned you into?" he cried out.

Then Rowan turned to look at Gavaah. He knew what he must do, and there wasn't a warrior in the kingdom who would stop him. He gently laid Mariah on the cart, then turned to face the evil lord. Fear filled Gavaah's eyes, and he began giving orders to his warriors as Rowan knelt down to recover his sword.

"What are you doing, Mosiah?" Lijah asked.

"My duty," Rowan replied.

"You will die," Lijah said.

Rowan looked at Lijah, bitter tears fueling the fire of revenge. "I am already dead!"

Lijah grabbed Rowan's arm, but before either of them could speak again, the crowd began to shout. Hundreds began to point at Gavaah and scream at him. The anger of the crowd flowed around the stands like a violent windstorm, and in moments the stadium had become a seething bed of uncontrollable rage. People began to pour out of the stands into the arena and run toward the grandstand.

Gavaah shouted for his warriors and sentinels to gain control, but they found themselves at the mercy of the angry mob. Pandemonium filled the arena, a chaos an army would be challenged to control.

Rowan and Lijah watched in shock as the events unfolded. Then Lijah leaned close to Rowan. "This is our only chance. If you want Mariah's death to count for something more noble than a failed attempt at revenge, then come with me, my brother."

Rowan looked down at the pale face of his love and knew that Lijah was right. Mariah would want so much more for him than Gavaah's death. She always had been the noble one. He leaned down and kissed her once more. Lijah pulled at him, and Rowan found it nearly impossible to leave her.

"Now, Rowan!" Lijah screamed above the shouts of thousands. Rowan slowly straightened, then disappeared with Lijah into the mass of people—people stirred to rage by the injustice of a tyrant.

They were almost to an open gate when Rowan stopped. He turned to see the body of his love once more, but thousands of angry men storming the grandstand impeded his sight. All he saw was the cart being jostled and moved as the storm passed by.

Rowan turned to follow Lijah out of the stadium and came face to

face with two large warriors. Certain these were two of Gavaah's hench-
men, Rowan hefted his sword, ready for a fight. But the warriors looked
beyond Rowan and Lijah and stepped aside to let them pass.

"Quickly!" one of them said.

Rowan raised an eyebrow at Lijah; then the two men passed the
warriors by, glancing behind as they went. Rowan saw one of Gavaah's
warriors working his way through the crowd and coming toward them.
The Silent Warriors ducked into the mass of bodies and disappeared.
Rowan and Lijah wasted no time in continuing their exit.

Outside the stadium, the pandemonium had spilled out into the
streets. Angry and panic-stricken people were running everywhere while
sentinels descended on the stadium from every direction. It was as if the
entire city had erupted out of control.

Rowan and Lijah found two horses running loose, reins trailing, evidently from sentinels the mob had unseated. The brothers mounted and
raced south through the streets of Kroywen. With Gavaah's sentinels
focused on the chaos of the stadium, Rowan and Lijah were able to
make the city limits with just two minor encounters.

That day marked the end of tournaments in Cameria and the beginning
of total oppression of the people. Gavaah survived the day and began to
rule with an iron fist, choking the remaining spirit out of the good
people of Cameria. The age of darkness was upon the kingdom, and
many longed for the days of old—days when the Code and the Prince
ruled the hearts of people and not the fear and oppression of an evil
tyrant. For the Knights of the Prince, however, one hope and promise
remained.

For many years ago, when the Prince came to Arrethtrae, He told
His knights there would be a time of great trouble.

"And when it comes," He said, "do not be afraid. For in the midst
of this great trouble, I will come for you."

NINETEEN

CALL OF
THE PRINCE

 Rowan and Lijah rode until Kroywen was far behind them. Rowan aimlessly followed Lijah, not caring where they went. His mind was forever filled with the anguish of Mariah's last few moments of life. He constantly fought the urge to return to her, even though he knew she was gone.

Lijah made no attempt to console Rowan. There is a pain so great that silent companionship is the only appropriate response, and that is what Lijah offered him.

They rode until it was too dark to continue. Lijah led them into the shadow of a small grove of trees, and they dismounted. They did not eat, but simply lay down on the thick grass and allowed the blackness of night to swallow them.

Rowan found sleep elusive. Tears for his beloved Mariah fell from the corners of his eyes long into the night as he wondered why his life seemed to be filled with such great contradictions of joy and pain. Eventually his body could endure the exhaustion of the day no more, and the elixir of sleep gave him a short reprieve from the anguish of his now-empty life.

In the morning, Rowan awoke to the smell of wild game being roasted on a small fire. Lijah sat across the fire, staring at him. His face was grim, and Rowan saw the pain in his eyes. Rowan sat up and blinked the sleep from his own.

"I am sorry, Mosiah," Lijah said. "I truly am sorry."

Rowan gazed into the fire for a long while. "Where do we go now?" he finally asked, trying to keep horror at bay.

"When you are ready, there is only one place for us: Chessington."

Rowan didn't need to hear Lijah speak it. Somehow he knew what needed to happen. It seemed he had known it for years. He felt like a droplet of water that had fallen on a mountain. No matter which way it turned or how long it took, the droplet would eventually fall into the Great Sea. Just as, inescapably, he and Lijah would end up in Chessington.

After eating, they mounted up and rode southwest toward the Altica Valley. Once again, they spent the day in silent travel. Rowan replayed the events of the previous day a thousand times, not because he desired to but simply because his mind could not keep from returning to Mariah. Questions about purpose, duty, and truth began to fill his mind.

After hours of travel, Rowan found himself frustrated, angry, and bitter once again. He even began to have doubts about the Prince Himself. Did He even care that so many had died or were held captive... seemingly for nothing?

By early evening, Rowan and Lijah had passed beyond the borders of Cameria. They camped along a river on the eastern edge of the great valley. Lijah was successful at spearing one small fish from the river, which made for a meager one-course meal.

They didn't hear the horses until it was much too late to hide. Rowan and Lijah jumped to their feet and drew their swords. The setting sun made it difficult to see, but Rowan could make out eight mounted men coming directly toward them from the west. He conjectured that this was a search party looking for the two traitorous men who had disrupted a city and brought chaos to Lord Gavaah's stadium.

Within just a few moments, Rowan and Lijah stood facing a towering wall of warriors and steeds. These did not look like Gavaah's sentinels or ordinary knights. They were too massive, too powerful.

The lead warrior scrutinized Rowan and Lijah, then pointed to the far side of their camp. Two warriors broke off to the left, and two broke off to the right, circling around behind them. Rowan and Lijah instinctively positioned themselves to cover each other's backs.

"Do not be alarmed," the leader said in a deep, commanding voice. "We are not here to fight you." He made a sweeping motion with his hand, and the circle of eight warriors spread outward from the camp and assumed a guardian's stance.

Lijah relaxed and lowered his sword. "I am Sir Lijah of Chessington," he said to the leader. "This is my brother, Sir Mosiah of Laos."

The leader's eyes narrowed, and he nodded once, then joined his brethren. Rowan gazed uneasily around the perimeter of their camp, where he could just barely see the huge warriors standing guard.

"What's happening, Lijah?" Rowan whispered.

"They are Silent Warriors, messengers of the King," Lijah was also watching carefully. "And I don't know what's happening."

From the same direction the warriors had come, Rowan heard the hoofbeats of a galloping horse. Chills went up and down his spine as a man on a brilliant white steed rode into the camp. He reined in the powerful animal and looked down on Lijah and Rowan. Rowan gazed up at the man and became lost in the glow of his nobility.

For a moment, the pain of yesterday faded away as he wondered at the man. Something told him he commanded more than these eight powerful warriors—he was a commander of legions. And yet there was something more than simply the air of command about him. Rowan had never seen him before...or had he?

Out of the corner of his eye, Rowan saw Lijah fall to his knees. Only then did he finally realize what was happening. Here before them, on the fringe of the Altica Valley, was the Son of the King...the Prince. This was no dream, but a shining reality.

Rowan felt strength leave his legs, and confusion swept over him. He knelt and bowed his head in submission to the One who had come to defeat the very enemy that had taken his love.

Rowan heard the Prince dismount and walk toward them. Seconds later, he felt a strong but gentle hand on his shoulder. "Rise up, My faithful knights." The voice was deep and warm.

Lijah stood up, but Rowan could not. His heart was broken and his vision obscured. The Prince knelt down close to him, placing both hands on his shoulders. Rowan lifted his head, and tears spilled from his eyes.

"I'm sorry, my Lord," Rowan's voice quivered. "The ache in my heart is too strong for me to be what You want me to be."

The Prince gazed into his eyes with such deep compassion that Rowan did not want to turn away.

"Your grief is great, as is Mine for you," the warm voice said. "The evil of Lucius has robbed the kingdom of so many noble men and women. I need you to help Me stop him. The memory of Mariah cries out for justice, as does the memory of all those who sacrificed in Cameria, and the day is near when I will return with My army to give them that justice. Until then you must stand strong. But you must do it in My strength, not your own."

Rowan needed the comfort of a father, someone to lean on and trust that all would eventually be all right. Somehow the Prince was this and more for him. How could this be?

Rowan lowered his head and leaned into the Prince. His forehead pressed against the chest of the Prince, and he felt the Prince's arm about his shoulder.

"Will you trust Me, Rowan?" The question was simple. Rowan realized that no matter the circumstances of his life, his belief in the Prince was the only treasure Lucius could never steal from him.

"Yes," he whispered, "I will trust You, my Prince."

The Prince allowed Rowan a moment to recover, then gripped his hand with His own and pulled him up. He then turned to Lijah.

"Lijah, I have watched you from when you were just a lad. You have been steadfast, faithful, and true, and you did not rest until you found your brother." The Prince put a hand to Lijah's chest. "In here beats a heart after the King's own."

Lijah bowed his head, clearly moved by the Prince's affirming words, and Rowan felt a twinge of shame for having doubted that this loyal and courageous knight was his brother. In that moment, he felt the true bond of brotherhood solidify, and it strengthened his heart.

"Come, My friends," the Prince said. "Walk with Me, for we have much to talk about."

Rowan and Lijah followed the Prince out of the small grove of trees and up a grassy knoll that looked out across the vast expanse of the Altica Valley. The sun was sinking far to the west, painting the sky in vibrant hues of blue, orange, and red. The Prince looked southwest, and Rowan knew He was thinking of Chessington.

"My words are for you and you alone. Speak them to no one." The Prince turned to face them. "I have given many brave men and women missions of great importance…and great danger. But what I am asking of you transcends anything I have asked of any of them. You two were born into the lineage of the King and have been equipped to do what no other could do."

Rowan looked over to Lijah, who caught his eye and nodded as the Prince continued. "The King's people in Chessington have rejected Me. Because of this, My Father has chastened them over the years, and they have endured great hardships. Meanwhile, Outdwellers throughout the kingdom have heard and believed in Me. The Knights of the Prince who are left in Chessington are being persecuted and imprisoned, but their swords still fly against evil and their testimony is reaching many—but they cannot do what I am sending you to do."

The Prince paused.

"The time has come to return the promise of the King to My people…and you shall be My voice. Before the end of days, because of your testimony, many will come to believe in Me as the Son of the King, and thousands will be spared a great reckoning."

"My Lord," Rowan asked, "how can this be such a great danger…or more of a mission of importance than You have asked of any other?"

The Prince hesitated. "Because many will believe you, but many will also despise you, and you will be in the vortex of a great evil. The Rising of Lucius has come, and the time of judgment is near. The people will be given one last chance to decide who has their allegiance."

The Prince looked out across the great valley once again. "Arreth-trae, and Chessington in particular, is on the precipice of great evil and great judgment, and you will be in the center of it all. Many will try to kill you for speaking the truth about Me. Alexander Histen's power is great in the land and will be greater, but I send you to be a stumbling block for him."

The Prince looked back and set His gaze upon the two brothers. "Rowan…Lijah…you are mighty men prepared for this day. Will you be My voice in Chessington, bringing many to the King through My name?"

Rowan and Lijah simultaneously knelt again before the great Prince. "We will, my Lord," they replied in unison.

"Then rise and drink from My flask of the bitter wine. The Life Spice within will give you strength to stand in the days to come."

Rowan and Lijah stood as the Prince lifted a leather strap from around His neck. On the strap hung a smooth leather flask, which He handed to Rowan. Rowan lifted the flask to his lips and drank. The wine tasted sweet in his mouth, but when he swallowed, it became bitter in his stomach, and he winced. He handed the flask to his brother, and Lijah did the same.

The Prince took back the flask and tucked it away in His tunic. "Now take that which you were given as infants, and journey due west across the valley to the foothills of the Northern Mountains. Follow the rivers north until you come to the place of beginnings. There you will clad yourselves in the armor of the King—in defense against the swords and arrows of Lucius. For a time, none shall overcome you while you proclaim Me to the people of Chessington!"

Rowan heard the pounding of many hoofs behind them. The mounted warriors of the Prince thundered up the knoll, bringing the Prince's white stallion with them.

The Prince put His hands on their shoulders. "Do not be afraid, for I will be with you to the end."

The Prince took the reins of His horse from the nearest warrior and quickly mounted. He raised His hand over the brothers, then turned and led the contingent of Silent Warriors west into the Altica Valley. Rowan and Lijah stared after them for a long while, until their hoofbeats faded into the shadows of the closing day. When they returned to their camp, fresh venison hung from a tree limb, and a basket of vegetables was waiting near the fire. They feasted and replenished themselves with the food of the Prince.

Afterward Rowan looked across the fire at his brother. "Lijah, I owe you an apology and a great debt of gratitude. Forgive me for not believing you."

Lijah nodded.

"And I want to thank you for risking your life to save mine…even when I didn't believe you. I hope that I can someday be as noble a brother to you as you have already been to me."

Lijah pushed to his feet, and Rowan did the same. Rowan offered his arm, and Lijah took it. It was the beginning of a bond that a legion of Shadow Warriors could not break—two mighty brothers fully committed to the Prince.

When they prepared their bedrolls that night, they were satisfied, anticipating the journey ahead. But sleep was a long time coming for Rowan.

"What is the place of beginnings, brother?" Rowan asked as he lay beside Lijah in the darkness.

"It is that place where Sir Peyton and Lady Dinan long ago ruled the kingdom," Lijah answered sleepily. "Nedehaven."

"Nedehaven," Rowan mouthed the word to himself, remembering the story Sir Aldwyn had told him early in his training. The fall of Nedehaven is what had eventually brought the Prince to Arrethtrae.

Rowan stared up at the stars for a long time that night, contemplating many things. When he thought of Mariah, the ache in his bosom threatened to overwhelm him. Had he failed her, failed them both? What if this new mission met the same fate as the last one? How could he and Lijah possibly prevail against the evil they were facing?

Then he seemed to hear the voice of the Prince once more, whispering in his ear, "You must do it in My strength, not your own… Trust Me."

And Rowan whispered once more as sleep finally came to him, "Yes, my Prince. No matter what happens…I will trust You."

TWENTY

THE ARMOR
OF THE KING

 It took Rowan and Lijah two long days to cross the vast Altica Valley and make their way into the foothills of the Northern Mountains. On the evening of the second day, they reached a wide river that Lijah called the Frates and made camp beside it. The next morning they found a place to ford the river and traveled north along its banks toward the confluence of the Frates and Tisgri rivers. Lijah seemed to know the way, and Rowan found himself content with following.

By early afternoon, they came to an area that seemed forgotten by time itself. It was a scene of ancient beauty. The Tisgri flowed nearby, tumbling gently over shallow waterfalls. The trees seemed larger than usual and widely spaced, and the ground between them was padded with thick grass and soft mats of forest moss. Green vines and brightly colored flowers provided a garden atmosphere, and a canopy of leaves and pine branches filtered the sunlight into golden spires.

They walked quietly through the trees until they came to the ruins of a forgotten estate. The outer walls had crumbled, and the rusted iron gates had fallen from their hinges. Rowan and Lijah walked through the gate and stood in the outer court of what once must have been a majestic palace. The trees and vines had nearly swallowed the blackened structure, and it looked as though it were trying to return to nature, but its residual magnificence was unmistakable.

"Nedehaven," Lijah breathed. "It must be."

"But how could there be anything of worth for us here?" Rowan asked.

Lijah shrugged. "It seems unlikely, but let us look just the same."

They combed the ruins for several hours and found nothing. Finally, Lijah sat down on a fallen stone slab that sank deep into the soft ground, as if the vines and moss were gradually pulling it under.

"Can you imagine the splendor of such a place before Lucius came to destroy it?" Lijah asked, sweeping his gaze across the ruins.

Rowan came to sit beside him, but with his last step his foot sank deeper into the moss than before. He pushed harder with his foot and realized the moss had overgrown a void at the base of the stone Lijah was sitting on.

"What is it?" Lijah asked.

"I'm not sure." Rowan knelt down to the impression in the moss. He dug in with his hand and began peeling back the thick layer of moss.

"Look, Lijah." Rowan peered down through the small hole he'd dug. "I think this stone you're sitting on is covering a stairwell."

Lijah knelt to look and help pull back the moss. They were able to uncover a portion of the first step to what looked like a circular stone staircase.

"It makes sense," Lijah said. "This would more than likely be the location of the great hall. We'll need to move this slab."

The stone was too heavy for even these two powerful men, but they were able to leverage a timber into the hole and slide the stone far enough off the steps to allow them to crawl through the opening. The light from the opening wasn't enough for them to see beyond a few steps, so they fashioned a couple of torches from a portion of a horse blanket and sticks. Setting them aflame, they started down the staircase.

At the base of the stairs, they found themselves in a hallway that led to numerous chambers. All of them looked strangely untouched by the tragedy that had happened above so long ago, but there was nothing of significance for Rowan and Lijah. At the end of the hall, they came to another staircase that led deeper into the ground. Rowan was a little unnerved as he looked down the steps that seemed to be swallowed up by the blackness. Lijah didn't hesitate, however, and Rowan followed him down.

At the bottom of this staircase was a single door. It took both of them to force the door open, for it was heavy, and the rusty hinges creaked in defiance of the movement. They entered the chamber and immediately knew there was something special about it. The chamber was empty except for a monolithic square column in the center. Embedded in the column was a metal plate with a small opening that looked like a keyhole.

The flames of their torches flickered off the walls of the chamber, and Rowan's threatened to die out soon. He looked at the dancing shadows that fell across Lijah's face.

"One marked child with a key," Rowan said, reciting the words from Lijah's scroll that Mariah had read.

Lijah took a deep breath. He lifted the key from around his neck and looked back at Rowan. It appeared to be a perfect fit.

Lijah put the key in the lock and turned it. The click of the lock echoed in the room, but that was all…at least at first. A few seconds later, something rumbled beneath their feet, and then Rowan heard the sound of large iron rods sliding across granite. Escaping air filled the room, and puffs of ancient dust shot from the corners of the far wall. Rowan heard something akin to a gate winch rumbling; then slowly the far wall began to sink into the floor.

As the upper portion of the wall dropped down, Rowan could see a void beyond it. He held his guttering torch up higher, and the weak light spilled into another chamber behind the descending wall. Within a few moments, the wall had disappeared into the floor, and both men stood in wonder at the hidden chamber before them.

It was circular in shape, approximately fifteen paces in diameter and equally as tall. Eight massive marble plates hung around the perimeter of the room, each one framed by elaborate moldings and bracketed by sconces holding large, ornate oil lamps. Lijah lit one of the lamps, and

Rowan did the same. There was enough light to see that this chamber had been fashioned by craftsmen of remarkable skill. They finished lighting the lamps and gazed around them, awed by the chamber's beauty.

Rowan walked over to one of the marble plates, his eyes fastened on an exquisitely carved image. It was a detailed scene of a battle between great warriors. Chills ran up and down his spine as he took it in. Rowan put his hand up to touch one figure that stood majestically above the rest. Across a gulf stood another figure equally as powerful, but with a countenance that portrayed a darkened heart.

Rowan went from plate to plate, mesmerized by each one. Each portrayed a grand scene of apparently supreme significance, although the two men could only guess what the significance might be.

"Mosiah," Lijah called.

Rowan broke his gaze from a plate that depicted a strangely familiar city on a hill skirted by a sea. He walked to the plate that Lijah was inspecting. Two knights wielding swords stood back to back, locked in mortal combat against a seemingly endless sea of enemies. Below the carving were words he had seen before.

"It's the verse from the scroll your mother gave you," Rowan said.

Lijah nodded. Rowan began to read it aloud.

Farewell peace on the river, farewell peace one and all,
Fear not dark in the evening; hear the Prince and His call.
Two babes born in sorrow—a husband weeps for his wife—
One child raised by his people, one child raised in strife,
One marked child with a key, one marked child will roam,
One marked child with an image, one marked child comes home.
The Code, the Key, and the Image, a chamber revealed for two.
A mission beckons My people. Words of the Prince be true.
Two men chosen in armor, abandoning life for the call.
Two men face the Dark One: to Chessington herald and fall!

Rowan slowly turned and looked at his brother. His grave countenance perfectly expressed what Rowan felt in his heart. Lijah reached out his hand and touched the last word of the verse.

" 'Herald and fall,' " Rowan repeated. "What does it mean, brother? Are we being sent to our deaths?"

"The Prince said He would be with us to the end," Lijah said quietly.

"Yes," Rowan mused, "but what if Chessington is our end?"

Lijah slowly turned his head and looked at Rowan. "Then I can think of no better way to die than in service to our great King," he said, his voice building confidence with each word.

Rowan didn't know how to respond.

Lijah put a hand on his shoulder. "Through the ages, everything the King and His Son have promised has come true, and they have promised the people victory over the Dark Knight and his Shadow Warriors. If we fail in this mission, thousands…perhaps tens of thousands will die from his evil hand."

Lijah paused and Rowan thought on his words.

"To fall can mean many things, Rowan. But if it should mean we die that many others might be saved, then give me ten deaths to die, that all the more might be saved."

Rowan could not help the smile that crept across his lips. "I am honored to be your brother, Lijah. I doubt there is another knight in the entire kingdom with a heart like yours."

Lijah met Rowan's eyes, and a subtle grin flashed across his usually somber face. Then he turned his eyes back to the inscribed verse. " 'One marked child with an image,' " he read out loud. "I guess it's your turn."

Rowan shook his head. "Even if I have an image, how could that help us?"

"I don't know," Lijah replied. "But there must be more reason for us to be here than to discover the last few words of the verse. Are you sure you weren't given an image of some sort?"

Both men turned their eyes back to the marble plate. "Just a birth-mark that Mariah—"

Rowan's gaze fell once more on the scene of knights in combat and he froze. On the armor of one of the knights was an image he had seen before. It looked just like the sketch that Mariah had drawn of his birth-mark that night back in Eagle's Nest.

Rowan reached out to trace his finger around the image on the marble and then pushed. That portion of the marble plate receded inward, and the entire plate began to descend into the floor, just as the wall had done.

What was revealed this time left both of the brothers in awe. The light from the chamber spilled into an alcove that held two magnificent suits of armor and two swords of un-Arrethtraen beauty. Rowan lifted one of the helmets from the armor display stand and held it aloft, amazed at how light it was.

"Remarkable." Lijah inspected a pauldron that guarded a shoulder of the other suit. "I've never seen anything comparable in Arrethtrae, and this is ancient."

Rowan placed the helmet on his head and lifted the visor. It was a perfect fit. "I don't think this was made in Arrethtrae," he said.

Lijah looked over at him and nodded. They donned the armor and lifted the swords and scabbards from their stands in the alcove, then fastened them to their belts. They twisted and turned, enjoying the flexibility and light weight of the armor. Then a silence seemed to fall upon them, and they turned slowly to face each other.

Lijah nodded solemnly at his brother. "Are you ready for this?"

Rowan nodded.

"Our mission begins now"—Lijah extended his arm—"and Chessington awaits."

Rowan grasped his brother's arm with an iron grip. "To Chessington."

TWENTY-ONE

CHESSINGTON'S PROMISE

 The journey to Chessington took many days. The farther south they journeyed, the more oppressed the people seemed to become. The closer they came to Chessington, the more Rowan felt as if they were slowly entering the lair of a dragon.

Each village they entered seemed crowded with skulking men that Rowan was certain were the wicked servants of Lucius, the Vincero Knights. He and Lijah even began to see Shadow Warriors, who did little to hide their identity. Rowan was at first alarmed by their bold appearances, but then he found himself growing indignant. What had begun as a mission of obedience was becoming a true passion of his heart.

When they reached Bremsfeld, Rowan and Lijah tarried there and began to proclaim the Prince to the people on the street who would listen. Crowds gathered, and the people responded dramatically to their bold words. Some cheered, some jeered. A few actually fled with haunted looks on their faces, but more replaced them. After just two hours, it seemed as if the entire town had gathered to hear these two gallant knights speak powerful words of warning, chastisement, and hope.

When they began to denounce the tyranny of Alexander Histen, the city officials became concerned and sent guards to quiet them, but they would not be quieted. Their passion for the Prince welled up to an unstoppable outpouring of truth.

When they would not remain quiet, eight guards approached with swords drawn. The crowd became alarmed, shouting both blessings and curses at the brothers.

Rowan pointed at the town prefect. "Recall your men, or the sword of the Prince will be against you!"

The prefect sneered and ordered his men to disarm Rowan and Lijah and take them into custody, but that is not what happened. The brothers drew their swords, and the crowd drew back. The guards advanced, but only momentarily. Rowan and Lijah made quick work of the first four guards. The other four pulled back, dragging their wounded comrades with them. Rowan saw fierce-looking men observing from afar.

By this time it was apparent that the people were no longer listening. Rowan and Lijah exchanged a glance, then turned to mount their horses.

"Hear the words of the Prince, people of Bremsfeld," Rowan shouted above the roar of the crowd. "Those who follow the Prince shall receive His reward, but those who deny the truth of His throne are enemies of the King."

Then he kicked his horse, and the two brothers rode out of Bremsfeld.

And so they continued their journey south through towns and villages, dividing the hearts of men and women by their bold proclamations. A trek that might have taken but four days became a mission unto itself, for Rowan and Lijah could not shut up their passion for the Prince.

Three more weeks they sojourned in the lands north of Chessington, stopping to speak in Keighwick, Attenbury, Chandril, and many a smaller village. Word of their mission spread across the kingdom before and behind them until the blaze of their words swept across much of Arrethtrae.

The message of the brothers drew many to the Prince and offended even more, for to hear them speak demanded a response from the souls of those who heard, a response to either follow or reject the Prince. Numerous times they were confronted by guards, Vinceros, and even Shadow Warriors, but none could stand against them, for they wielded their swords as the Prince Himself had, and the armor of the King was impenetrable.

As the days went by, they also began to realize they were not alone. News of the Resolutes' battle in Cameria had already swept through the kingdom, and Rowan was moved to see Knights of the Prince emerge and rally in response to that courageous stand. The Resolutes' example added fuel to Rowan's own purpose as well, and he resolved that the sacrifice of his friends—of his own beloved Mariah—would not be in vain. In his own mission he carried theirs as well.

After the fourth week of travel since leaving Nedehaven, they crested the northern rim of the Chessington Valley. Chills flowed up and down Rowan's spine as he beheld the great city of the King far below them.

Just beyond the city, over the waters of the Great Sea, rolling thunderclouds flashed lightning back and forth across the sky. A storm was coming. And if the Prince's words were true, a great storm was coming to Arrethtrae. Standing here, Rowan could sense the terrible evil that had the city in its thrall. And yet he could feel something else…a deep yearning of the King's people to hear the call of the Prince.

"Where there is great evil, there is even greater good," Sir Aldwyn had told Rowan once when he was just a boy. At this moment, looking down on Chessington, Rowan felt the truth of that statement in his very bones. Never before in the kingdom of Arrethtrae had people known such tyranny, but that very tyranny made them ache for that greater good…for Him whom they had rejected…for a perfect and good King.

Rowan looked over at Lijah. In the few weeks that they had journeyed, proclaimed, and fought together, he had come to know his brother more deeply than brothers who had lived a lifetime together, and he was grateful for the opportunity to stand beside such a man.

Lijah looked back at Rowan. The soberness of their duty and the reality of what it meant to the lives of countless others in the kingdom stole away their smiles, but not their joy.

"The people of the King are waiting," Lijah said quietly.

Rowan nodded. "Give me ten deaths to die!"

They spurred their horses and rode forward fearlessly toward the city that seemed to hold the future of the kingdom.

Rowan had never visited Chessington, but from the moment he and Lijah rode into the outskirts of the legendary city, he felt strangely at home—like he belonged there. And yet the city felt strange as well, as if hung with an aura of gloom.

Word of their coming had clearly reached the people of Chessington, for many scooped up their children and scurried from sight while others ran from their shops and homes to the street hoping to see the two knights who had stirred the hearts of many and stood openly against Alexander Histen's oppression.

Rowan looked into the eyes of the people and saw himself in their past and in their future. He saw confusion, disbelief, despair, and great pain. It reminded him of the pain he felt at losing Mariah. Here, the people had suffered great loss, and it was the Dark Knight, Lucius, who had robbed them both.

There was a complete absence of joy, much as if perpetual night had fallen on the city. The iron shackles of a great tyrant had been locked upon their souls. Rowan and Lijah had seen firsthand a portion of Histen's evil, and if it had fallen as far north as Cameria, then the darkness of this man's heart was great indeed. He was certainly a man in league with the Dark Knight himself.

Rowan looked at Lijah and saw in his eyes the same fiery resolve that was rising in his own bosom. He knew what pride felt like and the ugliness it brought to one's spirit, but the determination that now governed his thoughts was nothing like the stubborn hunger for glory that had once driven him. He and Lijah had been given a mandate by the

Prince Himself. They would prevail in His strength, not their own, and neither the Shadow Warriors of Lucius nor the strong arm of Alexander Histen would stand in their way.

Before they had traveled far into the city, four guards approached them with the now-familiar request to present their travel papers.

"We have none," Lijah returned.

His terse reply seemed to offend the leader, and his hand fell to the hilt of his sword. One of the other guards leaned near to the leader.

"It's the two knights we heard of coming from Chandril," he said quietly.

The leader looked from Rowan and Lijah to his cohort.

"I don't care who they are," he snapped at the guard. "We carry the authority of Governor Supreme Alexander Histen." He turned to Rowan and Lijah. "You will follow us to the consulate and present proper iden- tification for travel papers in accordance with Governor Histen's edict." He hesitated a moment and then motioned for his subordinates to cir- cle behind the two knights.

"No," Lijah replied evenly. "We will not comply, for we do not rec- ognize Histen's authority here."

The guard turned back, nostrils flaring, seemingly at a loss as to how to respond to such blatant disregard for Histen's power. "You will relin- quish your swords and follow us!" he finally blurted out.

"We are here to proclaim the Prince to the people of Chessington and to destroy the works of Lucius," Rowan stated. "Those who oppose us and our mission are enemies of the King and will be dealt with as such!"

The leader and his men began to draw their swords, but Rowan and Lijah did not wait for them. Their swords were arcing toward the guards before the blades had cleared their scabbards.

After the first clash of steel, one of the guards was off his horse and another's blade was broken just forward of the handle guard, the blade falling harmlessly back in his scabbard. Then Rowan engaged a second man while Lijah took the leader. Within seconds, Rowan's opponent had backed away, and the leader's sword lay harmlessly in the dirt near the hoofs of his steed. He smartly backed away and rode off, an expression of shock on his face. The fallen man remounted his horse and galloped after the three other retreating men.

Rowan and Lijah rode to the city square and dismounted. They walked to the center of the square, where a massive oak tree stood. Rowan knelt down and reverently touched the ground beneath it.

"Is this the place?" he asked Lijah.

Lijah nodded almost imperceptibly. "This is the place."

"Here the Prince went to the tree an innocent man and paid our price." Rowan looked about and tried to visualize the thousands of people who had gathered to see the Prince's execution. He imagined a legion of Silent Warriors waiting to charge upon the foolish people at the sound of His voice...but the Prince did not call them. Instead He silently went to His death—beaten, bruised, and rejected.

That was not the end, however, for if Nedehaven was the place of beginnings, this was the place of new beginnings. The Prince yet lived. Rowan had seen Him with his own eyes, and he was humbled at the realization that he and Lijah had been called to prepare the way for the Prince's glorious return to reign in Arrethtrae. Ahead were days of great glory and days of great woe for many.

"Do you come from the King?" Rowan heard a young voice ask. He stood up and turned to see a boy of perhaps thirteen looking at him.

"We do," Rowan replied.

"We've waited long for a message from the King," the boy said plaintively. "Is there a message?"

The yearning for hope in the boy's eyes tore at Rowan's heart. "There is indeed a message from the King," he said. "Go and tell the people to come hear it."

The boy's eyes widened; then he turned and ran down one of the streets that opened onto the square, yelling for the people to come and hear a message from the King. Before long the people began to gather. A few pointed to Lijah and nudged each other, as if they recognized him.

Lijah walked over to the highest knoll in the square, just in front of the tree, and began to speak.

"Chessington, we are a chosen people. Long ago, when the kingdom turned against us and persecuted and imprisoned us, the King heard our cries and delivered us from the treachery of Fairos. Here He brought us to a land of great wealth and prosperity." Lijah held out his arms as if to embrace Chessington and the valley in which it lay.

"When we turned our backs on Him again and were carried into captivity by the Kessons to Daydelon, He had mercy on us and brought us back to this great city and rebuilt our homes once more. In spite of His faithfulness to us, you have once again rejected Him, and because of this, His judgment has come upon you!"

Lijah's strong words immediately caused a stir among the people. "Why this judgment?" one man yelled out. "How have we rejected Him?"

Rowan pointed at the crowd that now had grown to twice its original size. "You rejected the King when you rejected His Son—the Prince!" Rowan gestured to the tree. "Here you killed Him, and you have endured many years of strife because of it!"

The people stirred again—some to anger, some to confusion, a few to grief and mourning.

"I don't even know what you're talking about," cried one woman.

"Who are you to accuse us?" one called. "What gives you the right?"

Finally, one man at the front of the crowd fell to his knees with his arms outstretched. "We are weary and afraid, for our city has fallen into the hands of evil men. Help us—"

"Silence!" screamed a voice from behind the crowd.

The crowd gasped and fell silent as a force of twenty guards descended on the people. The crowd split open to make way for them to approach Rowan and Lijah.

"You are in violation of Governor Histen's edict and will be imprisoned until you are judged accordingly!" exclaimed the leader of this contingent, who wore the telltale Vincero medallion, the sign of the knights who served Lucius.

Silence hung in the air while Rowan and Lijah slowly drew their swords. The people began to back away, distancing themselves from Rowan and Lijah's impending doom.

"By the power of the King and of His Son, we will stand before the people of Chessington and proclaim the truth," Lijah shouted. "Retreat, or endure His judgment!"

No more words were exchanged. The Vincero Knight charged with his men against Rowan and Lijah, and the people gasped as the scene unfolded. Rowan and Lijah fought back to back against impossible odds, but Arrethtrae had never seen the skill, armor, and swords of such men in all its days. Their swords flew in a blaze of cuts and slices, methodically destroying the contingent of guards one and two at a time.

At one point in the fracas, Rowan engaged the Vincero and another guard simultaneously. Although the Vincero's skill was much greater than that of the other guards, within just a few moments, Rowan's blade had pierced him through. He stumbled backward and fell over the body of one of his men, never to rise again.

The fight continued until only five guards remained. The clashing of swords stopped suddenly as they came to the full realization of what they were facing. They slowly retreated away from the square, not daring to turn their backs on Rowan and Lijah.

The crowd gawked in the aftermath of the fight, slowly returning to Rowan and Lijah. But they did not cheer as one might expect. Instead, the tears flowed. The testimony, the swords, and the boldness of Sir Rowan and Sir Lijah shouted to the people that the King had not abandoned them, and many wept for their shame and their deliverance all at the same time.

"No one could do what you have done unless he comes in the power of the King," one man shouted.

"Tell us more about this Prince," another cried out. "Help us to believe."

Rowan and Lijah proclaimed the Prince to the people of Chessington, and many became Followers that day.

For many, it was a day of beginnings.

For others who chose to turn away, it was the beginning of the end.

TWENTY-TWO

THE FINAL STAND

For many days, Rowan and Lijah walked the streets of Chessington, openly proclaiming the Prince, and their presence fueled a firestorm of response. City officials were enraged. Knights of the Prince who had gone into hiding were inspired to reveal themselves. Hope took hold of some citizens, while others looked around them in fear. The cauldron of the times boiled hot with emotion.

Rowan and Lijah daily met the attacks of Vinceros and guards, but they triumphed over them time and time again. Their armor did not falter against the blades and arrows of evil men. They were aware, however, that there was more—and worse—to come. They saw Shadow Warriors lurking in every shadowy alcove and wondered when Lucius would unleash his minions to the battle.

Meanwhile, the fame of Sir Rowan and Sir Lijah spread throughout the land. People from the far corners of the kingdom embarked on pilgrimages to come and hear the profound and bold words of the two unconquerable Knights of the Prince who had defied Alexander Histen in his own city. As in the days of the Prince, there were many, both citizens of Chessington and Outdwellers, who came to accept Him as the Son of the King. Some refused and found themselves in a desolate place somewhere between an unfulfilled promise of their King and the tyranny of an evil man. Unfortunately, there were countless more who came to despise and hate Rowan and Lijah for the words they spoke. Day by day as the two bold knights stayed in Chessington, the fervor of the kingdom elevated.

Each evening, Rowan and Lijah returned to the tree in the central square, keeping watch through the night and sleeping in shifts. The citizens of Chessington brought them food and water, even though city officials forbade it. Every day their needs were provided for. Occasionally they journeyed out into the surrounding region and proclaimed the Prince to others, but they always returned to Chessington. They had no home, no bed, and no table to eat upon.

One morning, three weeks after their mission in Chessington began, a prominent-looking Vincero appeared with six guards in tow. Chin in the air, he announced, "Governor Supreme Alexander Histen desires an audience with you."

Lijah gazed at him and said nothing. The silence slowly crumbled the Vincero's arrogance until he began to look nervously about.

"We do not recognize Histen's authority," Rowan finally said.

"Nevertheless," the knight insisted, "his governorship would like to speak with you."

"We are here and will be here today, tomorrow, and each day after that," Rowan said. "We speak our words openly for all to hear."

The Vincero stared at them for a long moment, then huffed and turned away.

"When will our mission end, Lijah?" Rowan asked as the Vincero and his men departed. He was not weary—in fact, quite the opposite was true—but the kingdom seemed to be tearing itself apart, and he was curious about the days to come.

Lijah put a hand on Rowan's shoulder and offered him a gentle smile. "I don't know, my brother. Darker days are coming—that's for certain. The people of Chessington need the hope of the Prince to guide them through those days."

Rowan nodded, still wondering.

Then, that very afternoon, Alexander Histen himself came to them. Rowan had never seen the man before, and he could not deny that

Histen was much more than he had envisioned him to be. His muscular black steed snorted as he approached, shaking its harness as if it wanted to trample the brothers underfoot. Histen's regal-looking armor was elaborately trimmed in gold and silver, and a purple velvet cape fell from his shoulders to drape over the horse's massive hindquarters.

Clearly, this man was more than a crafty politician who had maneuvered himself into a position of power. He was also a man of means and seasoned in the art of war. For the first time since their mission began, Rowan had to steel his nerves against potential fear.

Histen gazed emotionlessly down at them for a moment, then slowly dismounted. Two of his warriors did the same. Histen's boots rang on the cobblestones as he walked slowly toward the brothers, and Rowan's heart felt darkness flow in and around him as the man approached. He stopped in front of Rowan and stared into his eyes.

The man was slightly taller than Rowan and just as muscled. His face was long and chiseled, with a narrow blade of a nose and an angled jaw. A prominent brow shaded black eyes that seemed to peer into the soul. Rowan shuddered, caught off guard by the probing evil in the man's stare.

Histen then turned toward Lijah. As they faced off, Rowan's thoughts turned to the day the Prince had encountered the Dark Knight when he first came to the kingdom so many years before. Had there been a face-off like this before that battle?

Slowly Histen turned his back on both of them and looked out at the crowd that had gathered. As he did so, the people turned away, shrinking back from his gaze.

Histen didn't even bother to turn his head as he spoke to Rowan and Lijah. "You two have caused quite a stir in my city…in my kingdom."

"This will never be your kingdom," Rowan said.

Histen froze, then spun about and lunged toward Rowan, stopping just inches from his face.

"I already own it, foolish knight." Histen's voice was low and menacing. "From Nyland to Cameria, from the Wasteland to Chessington—every castle, every lord, every city, town, and village—it is all mine!"

Lijah stepped toward Histen with his hand on his sword. Histen's two warriors advanced with their hands grasping the hilts of their swords. Muscles tightened, with another ferocious fight just one draw away.

Lijah scowled. "You will never own that which is the most precious to have."

"What is that?" Histen asked.

"The hearts of good people," Lijah said. "They will always belong to the Prince!"

Histen hesitated, then relaxed and backed away. His warriors took their cue and did the same.

"I don't need their hearts." Histen smiled coldly. "I'll just crush them one by one until none remain." He took a deep breath and sighed. "We could banter back and forth all day, I suppose, but what would it gain any of us?"

He raised a long finger to point at the brothers. "Do you really think I couldn't annihilate the two of you in an instant?" he chided. "I have—how shall I put it?—resources at my disposal that you can't even imagine. You are alive simply because I have not killed you yet."

Histen flashed a quick smile like the glint off a dagger. "You may have a thousand who support you, but I have hundreds of thousands who support me and hate you. Can't you feel it?" Histen turned about as if he were feeling rain falling into his open hands. "It's everywhere, and you can't stop it. But the truth is, I am weary of your tiresome rhetoric in my city and wish to be rid of you without causing such a dramatic stir among the people. So I have a proposal. I will give you two days to leave the city of Chessington, and I promise not to hinder your departure."

Histen crossed his arms, waiting for Rowan and Lijah to reply.

"We will not stop proclaiming the Prince in Chessington," Rowan said evenly. "And neither you nor your men nor even our deaths will stop the truth of the Prince!"

Histen scowled at Rowan and drew close to him once again. "You really don't know me or what I am capable of." His eyes narrowed briefly, and then he turned away. He walked to his horse and swung into the saddle, his velvet cloak swinging behind him.

"You've been warned." He wheeled the horse around. "Leave—or die!" With a clatter of ironclad hoofs on cobblestones, he left the square, his entourage following close behind.

Rowan stared after Histen. "Is he who I think he is?"

"Perhaps," Lijah replied.

Two days later, at nightfall, Rowan and Lijah heard the clash of swords in the distance.

"They are fighting for us." Lijah looked in the direction of the fight.

"Who, brother?" Rowan asked.

Lijah hesitated. "The King's Silent Warriors."

"How do you know?" Rowan asked.

"Because Histen has sworn to destroy us, yet we are still here."

Rowan swallowed hard as he imagined what they would face if the Silent Warriors failed to stave off Lucius's Shadow Warriors. These dark warriors were obviously the "resources" Alexander Histen had spoken of.

As the days wore on, Rowan and Lijah continued faithfully, and often they heard the sounds of an ancient battle nearby. For three-and-a-half months they proclaimed, defended, and gave honor to the Prince.

Finally, one cold winter morning, Rowan and Lijah woke to a day heavy with oppression. The clouds hung low in the sky as they walked the streets, ready to speak to any who would listen. But the attention of Chessington, along with the rest of the kingdom, had been captured by Histen this day. People were gathered on every street corner reading a proclamation that Histen's men had posted.

Rowan and Lijah joined a knot of citizens around a lamppost to read the new edict that was pinned there.

ATTENTION, CITIZENS OF ARRETHTRAE!

Governor Supreme Alexander Histen is hereby appointed King of Arrethtrae. All people will swear allegiance to King Alexander Histen and acknowledge his authority over all subjects by complying with the following proclamation:

1. All subjects will bow in the presence of King Alexander Histen.
2. All subjects will pay a permit fee to the king in exchange for the privilege of buying and selling goods in the kingdom of Arrethtrae. Upon the purchase of this permit, the king's insignia will be imprinted upon the subject's right hand. Any subject attempting to buy or sell goods without the imprint of the king will be punished.
3. No subject will acknowledge the existence of any authority other than King Alexander Histen. Violation of this order is punishable by death.
4. No subject is allowed to carry a sword without the explicit approval of the king. All swords will be collected within the next two days.
5. No subject is allowed to travel beyond the limits of the city they reside in without proper authorization from the king.
6. No subject is allowed to travel at night without proper authorization from the king.

Any subject who fails to comply with all points of this proclamation will be immediately punished.

All Hail King Alexander Histen!

"It *is* him," Lijah said.

"Histen is the Dark Knight," Rowan nearly whispered. "Lucius himself."

Rowan felt his bosom burn with fury, and he reached up to rip the proclamation from the post.

"People of Chessington!" he shouted. "Do not bow your knee to Histen, for he is a false king who has profaned the true King of Arrethtrae. The Prince is coming to rule the land, and Alexander Histen will be judged!"

The group around him seemed to dissolve as fearful people disappeared down the street.

"Come, let's return to the square," Lijah said. "Many will want to hear us this day."

The crowd had already gathered when they arrived back at the square—thousands of people waiting to hear the response of Sir Rowan and Sir Lijah to the new proclamation. But before they could begin, the thunderous clatter of many hoofs on cobblestones surrounded them. There was no warning except the drawing of hundreds of swords.

Rowan realized the hulking figures before them were not the guards they had faced so many times before. These were Lucius's Shadow Warriors, fighting now in the open with no regard for secrecy or discretion.

Rowan could see Lucius behind them, his countenance glowing with evil anticipation. The warrior force waded into the crowd, striking anyone who was in their way. People fled every which way, trying desperately to avoid the warriors' slashing blades.

Rowan and Lijah drew their swords as twenty massive Shadow Warriors surged toward them, with more behind. The Shadow Warriors seemed ruthless and fearless compared to their previous foes, but the two Knights of the Prince held strong, once again fighting back to back.

Rowan's mind flashed back to the marble plate that hung in the chamber at Nedehaven. The prophetic truth of that scene unfolded before him now.

They fought what seemed like an endless sea of monstrous warriors. Three warriors fell, then four, then five. Rowan drew his short sword to aid his efforts, and Lijah fought with two swords as well. The power of the King's steel vanquished foe after foe.

Through it all, Lucius watched smugly from atop his steed. By now the crowd had dispersed, and all the citizens were hiding.

Before the hour was half spent, more than eighty Shadow Warriors lay dead at the brothers' feet, but more were coming, and Rowan was tiring. Would this battle ever end? he wondered. Just when the fighting seemed to slow, Lucius raised his arm, and fifty more warriors appeared from behind him, running like hounds to a feast. Rowan's blade pounded like thunder from a storm, and Lijah fought with indomitable courage, but they slowly began to falter.

One blade crashed down on Rowan's shoulder so hard that he stumbled to his knee just as another cut pounded into his right side. He glanced quickly toward Lijah to see if there was any hope of help from him, but at that moment a sword blasted into Lijah's helmet and sent him to the ground. Rowan went to cover for Lijah while he tried to regain his feet, but the Shadow Warriors would not allow it. They brought an endless concussion of blows to the brothers' heads and chests until both men were pinned beneath an avalanche of dark grisly blades.

"Lijah!" Rowan screamed as one large Shadow Warrior plunged a spear with all his might down toward Lijah's chest. The spear broke in two as it collided with the King's armor, but not before its tip penetrated deep into Lijah's chest. Rowan tried to crawl toward his brother, but the boots of four men beat him back to the ground.

"Lijah!" Rowan screamed again.

"Brother," Lijah managed to call back, but his eyes began to darken.

"Fools!" Lucius approached them unhurriedly, drawing a sword whose flashing blade was engraved with the image of a dragon. "I am the ruler here, and there is no one to stop me—not even the messengers of the King!"

Rowan lifted himself up onto his elbow in an effort of defiance, but Lucius raised his wicked sword high in the air and plunged it downward with all his might. The dragon-decked blade pierced through Rowan's armor and plunged deep into his side. Pain seared through his body and mind, and he screamed against it. The Dark Knight's sadistic laugh added to the horror of the moment.

Lucius put his foot on Rowan's chest and yanked the sword from his body. Rowan crumpled to the ground, fighting for breath through collapsing lungs.

"I have defeated the King's messengers!" Lucius yelled. "I will rule both kingdoms, for I am greater than both the King and His Son!"

A cheer rose up from the darkened voices of a hundred Shadow Warriors. It seemed to echo to all four corners of Arrethtrae.

"Rowan," Lijah rasped.

Rowan was still an arm's length away. His arms and legs were heavy and growing cold, but he made a monumental effort to crawl to his brother. He reached out his hand and grasped Lijah's.

"The King reigns…," Lijah began, but then closed his eyes in death.

"My Prince…why have You forsaken us?" Rowan whispered. The light of the day began to fade. His eyes closed as a still, small voice whispered in his heart, "I am here."

Rowan's last thought was of holding Mariah in his arms. Then everything went dark. ◼

TWENTY-THREE

LIFE LIKE THE PRINCE

Lucius left Rowan's and Lijah's bodies in the square beneath the tree for all to see—evidence that he had overcome two of the Prince's mightiest warriors. Even those who had heeded their message dared not take the corpses for burial. They hid in their houses while the wicked men and women of the kingdom shouted and made merry over the news of the knights' deaths. But the celebration of evil did not last long, for Lucius and his minions did not realize that the Life Spice the Prince had given to Rowan and Lijah was working in the brothers' still forms.

Two days their bodies lay in the square for the people to scorn, but on the third day the people of the land trembled at the sight of the work of the King…a work that had not been accomplished since the day the Prince Himself conquered the treachery of Lucius and the taint of death.

"Rowan."

The sound was hollow and distant, and it seemed buried in the thunderous sound of an avalanche.

"Rowan."

Something now tugged on his hand, but his body seemed paralyzed, and he couldn't respond.

Rowan breathed, and it seemed as if it was the first time he had ever used his lungs. At first it hurt, but then the air seemed to cleanse his whole body. Not far away, he could make out the jeers of thousands of people laughing, screaming, and shouting obscenities against the King, the Prince, Lijah, and himself.

"Rowan," he distinctly now heard his name, and Lijah was calling it. Had the Shadow Warriors mistakenly left them alive?

"I am here, Lijah," Rowan said with difficulty.

"It is time to get up," Lijah said.

Rowan faintly remembered his final moments before losing consciousness and the extreme challenge he had in crawling just a few feet to Lijah. How could he possibly get up?

Rowan very slowly turned his head toward Lijah and saw they were still lying in the same position, Rowan's hand on top of Lijah's.

"Are you able, my brother?" Rowan said, now fully conscious and amazed that Lijah was still alive. "How can we yet be alive?"

"By the power of the King," Lijah replied. "The work of the Life Spice within us is complete, and it is time to get up. Our mission is accomplished, and the Prince is calling us home."

Rowan couldn't imagine being able to move, for Lucius's sword had pierced his side, and the pain before he fell unconscious had been unbearable.

Still… "I will try, my brother."

Rowan gathered himself for a moment, much as he did when lying in bed on a cold morning, waiting for the strength and will to rise.

"The King reigns," Lijah began once more.

"And His Son!" Rowan replied. At that proclamation, Rowan felt life pour into his bones and muscles. He sat up, and so did Lijah.

"Look!"

Rowan first heard a scream, then a collective gasp from thousands of lungs. "Impossible!" cried a voice. The shouts of alarm and exclamations elevated in volume.

Rowan lifted himself to one knee, fully expecting an avalanche of pain to cripple his efforts, but the pain did not come. He looked at Lijah and saw him, too, rise to one knee. Unspeakable joy filled his heart as the strength of his body returned to him. He reached out to Lijah, and the two brothers grasped hands. Together they rose to stand once more, their legs weak and shaking but gaining strength by the second.

The crowd was now in a state of sheer panic. People began to run every direction, screaming unintelligibly.

"Come, my brother," Lijah said. "He awaits."

Rowan and Lijah began walking south through the streets of Chessington, leaving a wake of shock on the face of every citizen who saw them. Some people fainted while others fell to their knees, begging the brothers not to harm them. A few shouted praises to the King, but they were few.

Thousands of astonished people followed Rowan and Lijah as they continued south toward the Great Sea. Finally they reached the docks of Chessington. Off the end of the longest dock, a grand ship was moored, ready to sail. Two mighty warriors stood side by side just before the gangplank. Their swords were drawn and ready as they waited for their precious cargo to arrive.

Rowan and Lijah approached the warriors and stopped just a few feet before them. Rowan recognized them as the two Silent Warriors they had briefly encountered when they were fleeing the stadium at Kroywen. The warriors lowered their swords and stepped aside, allowing Rowan and Lijah to board.

They walked up the gangplank and onto the deck of the gallant ship. Before them stood the One who had met them on the fringe of the Altica Valley months earlier…the Prince Himself. Both men fell to one knee before Him and lowered their heads.

Rowan felt the mighty hand of the Prince on his shoulder. "Rise, my good and faithful servants."

Rowan and Lijah stood and took in the warm glow of the Prince's gaze.

"My Lord," Rowan said, "we proclaimed Your name to all the people, and many became Followers, but many more would not listen."

"You have done well, Rowan and Lijah. The hearts of men and

women cannot be forced, only called, and that you have done. You sacrificed much, and great is your reward. Tonight I will gather the rest of My people, and we will all feast with My Father in the Kingdom Across the Sea."

"What of Lucius, my Lord?" Rowan asked. "And Gavaah in Cameria…and Malizimar in Daydelon…and the Shadow Warriors?"

"The days of Lucius and his Shadow Warriors are numbered." The Prince looked soberly past Rowan and Lijah to the city of Chessington and beyond. "I will return to conquer them, and you will reign with Me in the land. There shall be no end to My kingdom, and the people will prosper in peace."

The Prince dropped His gaze to the brothers and smiled. "But now is the time for your hearts to be filled with joy."

The Prince stepped aside and held out His arm toward the door of the main cabin ten paces away. One of the two Silent Warriors who had met them slowly opened the door, and Rowan held his breath as a vision of wonderment appeared before him.

"Mariah," he whispered, tears flooding his eyes.

His wife stood whole and beautiful, with her arms outstretched. They ran to each other, and Rowan threw his arms around her. He held her tightly for a long while.

"I've missed you so," she whispered.

Rowan breathed in the sweet fragrance of her hair, burying his face in its softness.

"Mariah," he said tenderly. "Praise the King you are here. Please don't ever leave me."

Mariah leaned back from him and put her hand to his cheek.

"Never, my love. Never again…forever!"

ACROSS THE GREAT SEA

There are those who die for the empty and worthless things of this kingdom, like silver, gold, and the acclaim of the crowds. There are those who die for noble reasons such as duty and honor. But there are a select few who will lay down their lives so that others might live. Such men were Sir Rowan and Sir Lijah. The courage they found through the Prince and the strength He gave them is far beyond anything this kingdom can understand. However, their kingdom is not of Arrethtrae, but of a place much greater.

The telling of the story of the great Sir Rowan is one that has hushed the tongues of babes to silence...one that gives occasion for us to pause and learn much. For in spite of the King's profound call upon his life, the great knight was nearly destroyed by the deceitful ploy of the Dark Knight. His collapse into pride was costly, for every dire vice brings dire consequences. And yet the King's ability to recover a heart that repents of even this great of an offense is not limited. Be encouraged, therefore, for though you may have failed the King, He will *never* fail you nor cease in calling you home.

On the day that Sir Rowan and Sir Lijah rose up and departed Chessington, the Prince sent forth His Silent Warriors as reapers throughout all of Arrethtrae to harvest the men, women, and children who had chosen to follow Him. Rowan and Mariah were jubilantly reunited that night with her father, Julian, and Sir Aldwyn. The silent exodus of many thousands was a time of great joy, as chronicled in previous parchments. But it was also a time of great woe, for the debauchery of Lucius, under the false name of Alexander Histen, went unabated, and his terror spread quickly throughout all four corners of the kingdom. Those left behind who did not bow or pledge their allegiance or take the Dark Knight's mark on their hand were beaten, jailed, and even executed. Lucius used fear to rule and forced all people in every region to submit to him as king of Arrethtrae.

It was a time of great despair, but the King did not let it last long. As Lucius reigned in terror, the Prince and His knights prepared to return and save the land once more.

Sir Rowan and Sir Lijah heard and submitted to the noble call of the Prince, sacrificing everything so that others might hear and live. I, Cedric of Chessington, am both honored and humbled to be given this weighty task of recounting the acts of such mighty men of valor. Their call was much like our own...to be witnesses for the great Son of a great King.

The chronicles of these and other mighty Knights of Arrethtrae are many, and there is not enough parchment nor ink in all the kingdom to record them. Alas, that which I have penned must suffice for now. My hope rests with you, courageous knight, that you will be inspired to live noble and true to the King and His great Son. And perhaps somewhere, someday, the chronicle of your life will be so grand that heralds will tell it in the halls of castles abroad. When you live for the Prince...anything can happen!

The King reigns...and His Son! 🔲

The story continues with *Kingdom's Reign*,
book 6 of the Kingdom Series.

DISCUSSION QUESTIONS

Review Questions from the Kingdom Series

Much of the allegorical symbolism in the Knights of Arrethtrae originated in the Kingdom Series. Here are a few questions to review this symbolism.

1. Who does the Prince represent?
2. Who are the Knights of the Prince?
3. Who are the King's people? the Noble Knights?
4. What is Chessington? Arrethtrae?
5. Who is the Dark Knight/Dark Lord/Lucius?
6. Who are the Silent Warriors and the Shadow Warriors?
7. What is a Vincero Knight?
8. What is a haven?

Questions for *Sir Rowan and the Camerian Conquest*

CHAPTER 1

1. Many people are extremely gifted with talents and abilities, but often those gifts are not used wisely and can even become an avenue of temptation. Find a verse in James 1 that explains where all good gifts come from. How do we guard our hearts against the temptation to use them wrongly?
2. At what point in this chapter does Rowan begin to falter in his integrity as a Knight of the Prince?
3. When does it become apparent that the draw of fame has taken hold of Rowan?

CHAPTER 2

1. In this chapter, we get a glimpse of how infatuated the people of Cameria have become with the tournament games. This is

symbolic of an overindulgent attitude toward any activity. Why can this become a problem for a nation?

2. Can you give an example of such a tendency in our own society?

3. When Rowan becomes successful as a tournament knight, his call to be a Knight of the Prince fades into the background and the tournaments themselves become his priority. What "seed" in the parable of the sower (Mark 4:3–20) represents Rowan's abandoning the Prince's call on his life for the fame and riches of the tournaments?

4. When Rowan wins the tournament, he receives a "victory cloak" which represents the vice of this book. What do you think this cloak represents?

5. Why is pride so dangerous?

Chapter 3

1. Rowan encounters a mysterious knight who defeats him in a contest. The duel ends with Rowan's cloak being cut and falling to the ground. Who do you think this mysterious knight is, and what does this scene represent?

2. What does James 4:6 say about God's response to someone who is sinfully prideful?

Chapter 4

1. Sir Aldwyn visits Rowan and confronts him about losing his way in regard to following the Prince. True friends lovingly tell us what we *need* to hear, not always what we *want* to hear. How did Rowan respond to Sir Aldwyn's confrontation?

2. Find at least one verse in Proverbs that warns about the consequences of a haughty spirit.

3. Have you ever had a friend lovingly confront you about a sinful attitude? What was your response?

4. Once again Rowan faces the mysterious knight, and once again he is defeated, with his cloak falling to the ground. The

knight warns Rowan to "turn back." How does God warn us to "turn back" when we begin to harbor a sinful attitude or behavior?

CHAPTER 5

1. How do the bandits on the roadway get Rowan to stop and talk to them? What is this called?
2. Have you ever been pressured into doing something wrong by someone who was appealing to your ego? How did you respond?
3. What is God's promise in Psalm 5:12 to those who live for Him?

CHAPTER 6

1. The beginning of this chapter gives a little bit of history regarding the United Cities of Cameria and the Prince. What do the United Cities of Cameria represent?
2. What does the support for Chessington by the United Cities of Cameria represent?
3. "Early on…being Camerian had been nearly synonymous with being a Follower." What assumption by many people of the world does this represent? Why is this assumption false?
4. What does Rowan's imprisonment and misery in captivity represent? (See Proverbs 16:18; 18:12; and 29:23.)
5. The moths and flesh-eating caterpillars represent how sin eventually consumes us, robbing us of our joy and strength. Find verses in Psalms that convey this truth.

CHAPTER 7

1. In this chapter, Rowan finally understands that his choice to follow the Prince was the most important thing he had ever done. What parable in the New Testament tells of a young man who "came to himself" as Rowan did?

2. Rowan begs for the Prince to forgive him for the foolish life he's lived. What promise does James 4:10 hold for those who humble themselves before the Lord?

3. Rowan encounters the Prince in a dream and realizes that He was the mysterious knight who had warned him to turn back. How is the Prince's approach to Rowan different this time? Find a scripture that indicates why.

CHAPTER 8

1. Rowan is delivered from the cave by Mariah, someone he'd never met before. Has God ever sent someone you did not expect to help you?

CHAPTER 9

1. Rowan ponders the question, *If the cost of such a [pure and humble] heart were all of my fame and wealth, would I make the trade?* This question alludes to Jesus' encounter with a rich young ruler. Find that Bible passage. What did Jesus have to say after the rich young ruler left? Can you find another passage where Jesus taught about wealth?

2. Rowan learns that Balenteen has betrayed him and taken his possessions. Have you ever been betrayed by someone you thought was a friend? Though it is difficult, Jesus tells us to forgive them if they repent (Luke 17:4). Have you been able to forgive?

CHAPTER 10

1. Rowan learns that his abduction and the takeover of Cameria are being orchestrated by Lord Malizimar because Cameria was supporting Chessington. What do you think this allegorically represents?

2. In this chapter we are introduced to the Resolutes. Who do you think they represent?

CHAPTER 11

1. A mysterious and mighty knight appears and saves Rowan, Mariah, and Zetta from the sentinels. He claims to be a Knight of the Prince, but he acts more like a Silent Warrior. His purpose seems different than most Knights of the Prince. What do you think his mission might be?

CHAPTER 12

1. The thieves intended harm, but Rowan and Mariah choose to demonstrate the compassion of the Prince by providing a meal for them. What verses in the Bible encourage us as believers to show the love of Christ in such a way?

2. Rowan and Mariah share the story of the Prince with the bandits. What command of Jesus does this suggest, and where do we get this command?

CHAPTER 13

1. Rowan is surprised at how many people have joined the Resolutes. Throughout time, God has preserved a remnant that has stayed true to Him even in difficult times. Find some biblical instances of this happening.

CHAPTER 14

1. Here we learn that a man by the name of Alexander Histen has risen to power and gained great influence throughout the kingdom. Who do you think this man might represent in the Bible? Give a Scripture reference.

CHAPTER 15

1. Rowan faces Sir Lijah and is confronted with the possibility that they are brothers with a different mission in Chessington. Lijah says that the events unfolding aren't about Laos or even Cameria but about Chessington. What portion of the story of mankind do you think this book is allegorizing?

2. What does Chessington represent, and why is this city so important?

3. Sir Lijah says that Rowan is one of the King's people, the descendants of Nan. What do you think this represents? Can you name which book in the Kingdom Series this reference comes from?

CHAPTER 16

1. What does the battle of Laos represent?

2. The battle for Laos fails, and most of the Resolutes are captured or killed. What does this represent in the end times? Give a Scripture reference.

CHAPTER 17

1. Lord Gavaah makes a proposal to Rowan that he momentarily considers. What helps him overcome the temptation to accept the offer?

2. Name some promises of God that can help us remember whom we serve and why.

3. When Gavaah explains his gruesome game for Rowan's and Mariah's lives, he indicates that the people love a bloody fight and want more because that is the way of the human heart. Do you think this is true? What can prevent a society from spiraling down like this?

CHAPTER 18

1. Mariah's apparent death crushes Rowan's heart, and his anger spurs him to revenge. What does the Lord say about vengeance in Deuteronomy 32:35?

2. Relate the final scene and conclusion of this chapter to the end times as foretold in Luke 21:10–34. According to John 14:27, what is the hope and promise of those who believe in Jesus?

CHAPTER 19

1. The Prince comforts Rowan in his great pain. How has God comforted you in your times of heartache? What are some Bible verses that provide comfort in times of need?

2. Standing on the edge of Altica Valley, the Prince gives Rowan and Lijah their mission, which parallels that of two men in Scripture. Who are these two men, and what is their mission as described in Revelation?

3. Some Bible scholars believe that the two witnesses of Revelation will be the same two men of the Bible who appeared on the Mount of Transfiguration in Matthew 17:1–3. Using the names Mosiah and Lijah as clues, can you figure out who they represent?

CHAPTER 20

1. At Nedehaven, Rowan and Lijah confirm their mission for the King and His call upon their lives. God calls each of us to specific forms of service and mission, but He does so in many different ways. Talk to someone in full-time or part-time ministry and ask how God specifically called him or her.

CHAPTER 21

1. In Chessington, Rowan and Lijah act on their mission to proclaim the Prince. According to Revelation 11, how long did the two witnesses have power to prophesy to the world?

CHAPTER 22

1. What does Scripture say will happen to the two witnesses when their mission of prophecy is complete? State the reference.

CHAPTER 23

1. One of the most profound sequence of events during the end times is the testimony, death, and resurrection of the two

witnesses, if indeed they literally represent two men. According to Revelation 11, how do the people of earth respond to their death?

CHAPTER 24 AND EPILOGUE

1. Rowan and Lijah are brought back to life through the Life Spice. What specifically does the Life Spice represent here? Find the verse in Revelation that supports your answer.
2. When Rowan and Lijah meet the Prince on the ship, Lijah asks about the fate of Lucius and his Shadow Warriors. What does the Prince say, and how does this relate to the end times? Read Revelation 19:11–20:3.
3. What book in the Kingdom Series tells the rest of the end times story?
4. Following Jesus Christ and walking in the Spirit can be the most exhilarating adventure of a lifetime. God wants to accomplish great things for His kingdom through us. Can you find a verse in John 14 that tells us of the great works we can do in the name of Jesus for God's glory?

ANSWERS TO DISCUSSION QUESTIONS

Answers to Review Questions from the Kingdom Series

1. The Prince represents Jesus Christ.
2. The Knights of the Prince represent all Christians.
3. The King's people represent the Jewish people. The Noble Knights represent the Jewish religious elite who were hostile to Jesus and His disciples (the Pharisees, scribes, etc.).
4. Chessington represents the land of Israel and also the holy city of Jerusalem, and Arrethtrae represents the whole world (*earth* and *terra* are combined backward to make up this word).
5. The Dark Knight, also referred to as the Dark Lord or Lucius, represents Satan.
6. The Silent Warriors are God's angels, and the Shadow Warriors are Satan's demons.
7. A Vincero Knight is a person who has been personally trained by one of Lucius's Shadow Warriors to spread and cultivate evil. Vincero Knights are ruthless and twisted by the evil that has mentored them. They represent people who are committed to propagating evil in the world, such as terrorists, murderers, drug dealers, and the like.
8. A haven represents a local church, where believers are trained, discipled, and sent out to share the gospel with others.

Answers to Questions for *Sir Rowan and the Camerian Conquest*

CHAPTER 1

1. James 1:17 says that every good and perfect gift comes from God. If we are careful to give God the glory in all that we do, we will not be as tempted to use our gifts and talents for the wrong purposes.

2. Rowan begins to falter when he enters a tournament against the wise counsel of Sir Aldwyn.

3. The draw of fame took hold when Rowan "reveled" in the glorious feeling of being victorious. Such experiences can be dangerous for a believer, since all glory should be given to the Lord. For Rowan, this is the beginning of a serious problem with pride.

CHAPTER 2

1. Often, when a nation begins to focus too intently on a particular recreational activity, more important work will be neglected. Unhealthy attitudes toward work and resources can become a way of life that is difficult to overcome.

2. Answers will vary.

3. Rowan's life is best represented by the seeds that were sown among the thorns, where the cares and deceitfulness of riches and the desires for other worldly things choke out the Word, as explained by Jesus in Mark 4:18–19.

4. The cloak represents Rowan's pride.

5. Pride is dangerous because it elevates oneself above others and even above God. Pride was the first sin and was committed by Satan when he determined in his heart that he would "be like the Most High" (Isaiah 14:13–14).

CHAPTER 3

1. The mysterious swordsman will be revealed later in the book. This scene represents the way the Lord chastens one of His children to correct a bad attitude. See Hebrews 12:5–7, 11.

2. God resists the proud but gives grace to the humble.

CHAPTER 4

1. Rowan became angry.

2. Proverbs 16:18 tells us that "destruction" and "a fall" will be the results of a haughty spirit. Other possibilities are Proverbs 18:12 and 29:23.

3. Answer based on personal experience.

4. God uses His Word, the Holy Spirit, parents, siblings, friends, and even circumstances to warn us.

CHAPTER 5

1. The bandits appeal to Rowan's pride. This is called flattery, and it is a very effective tool of the enemy. See Psalm 5:9 and Proverbs 26:28; 29:5.

2. Answer based on personal experience.

3. God promises blessing and protection like a shield.

CHAPTER 6

1. The United Cities of Cameria represent the United States of America.

2. This represents the United States' support of the nation of Israel today.

3. That statement represents the assumption that most Americans are Christians. This is false because being from a nation with a Christian heritage does not make one a Christian. Only a personal belief in Jesus Christ makes one a Christian.

4. This represents the "destruction" and "fall" of a man consumed by pride and a haughty spirit.

5. Psalm 31:10 (KJV); Psalm 38:3; and Psalm 51:8 are just a few examples.

CHAPTER 7

1. The parable of the prodigal son, told by Jesus in Luke 15:11–32, tells of a young man who "came to himself."

2. James 4:10 says that God will lift them up.

3. The Prince shows Rowan compassion and mercy and offers him forgiveness. The Bible says in Psalm 51:17 that God will not despise a broken and contrite heart.

CHAPTER 8

1. Answer based on personal experience.

CHAPTER 9

1. The Bible passage is Matthew 19:16–26. Jesus said that it is difficult for a rich man to enter into heaven. In Matthew 6:24, Jesus said that a person cannot serve both God and money. Any of us, no matter our financial status, can fall into this trap of choosing money as our lord instead of Jesus. Other verses relating to this are Luke 18:25; 1 Corinthians 1:26; 1 Timothy 6:9–10, 17–19; and James 1:11.
2. Answer based on personal experience.

CHAPTER 10

1. This represents the targeting of the United States by fanatical terrorist groups because of its support for Israel.
2. The Resolutes represent those who fight against the suppression of freedom and specifically religious freedom. As later chapters will show, they also represent the persecuted Christians in the end times who will wage spiritual warfare through prayer.

CHAPTER 11

1. Answers will vary. (His true identity will be revealed in later chapters.)

CHAPTER 12

1. Some possibilities are Matthew 5:44 and Luke 6:27–35.
2. This is an example of sharing the gospel of Jesus Christ with the lost, thereby fulfilling the Great Commission as given in Matthew 28:19–20; Mark 16:15; John 20:21; and Acts 1:8.

CHAPTER 13

1. Some examples are Isaiah 1:9; 10:22; Jeremiah 23:3; Ezekiel 6:8; Romans 9:27; 11:5; and Revelation 12:17.

CHAPTER 14

1. Histen represents the Antichrist, depicted in the book of Revelation (beginning in 13:1) as the "beast." (The actual term *antichrist* is introduced by John in 1 John 2:18, 22; 4:3; and 2 John 1:7.)

CHAPTER 15

1. This story allegorizes the days leading up to the end times as depicted in Revelation.

2. Chessington represents the nation of Israel. It is important because according to Scripture (for instance, Daniel 9:12), the end times will culminate in one of this nation's cities, the historic city of Jerusalem.

3. The King's people represent the Jewish people, descendants of Abraham who came from Canaan. The Kingdom Series book that first contained this symbolism is *Kingdom's Dawn*.

CHAPTER 16

1. The battle for Laos represents a spiritual battle in the end times when the Antichrist comes into power and begins to persecute the followers of Jesus.

2. Revelation 6:9 refers to "the souls of those who had been slain for the word of God and for the testimony which they held." (The intention of this story is not to place this passage within the context of a particular time frame, but rather to show that there will be difficult times for believers as the end times near.)

CHAPTER 17

1. Remembering the promises of the Prince helps Rowan overcome the temptation.

2. Some possibilities are Matthew 13:43; Psalm 34:17; and Deuteronomy 31:6.

3. Answers will vary. Jeremiah 17:9 says that "the heart is deceitful above all things, and desperately wicked." History has shown

that societies do tend to spiral down into wickedness and blood-lust, especially when they do away with God and His moral absolutes. Only principled, moral, and godly men and women leading a God-centered people can keep this from happening.

CHAPTER 18

1. Deuteronomy 32:35 says that vengeance belongs to the Lord (not to us!) and that He will repay the wrongs done to us.
2. Jesus tells us that in the end there will be distressing times but that we will be a testimony for Him, just as the Knights of the Prince are for the Prince. Just as they hope for the Prince's return, our hope as believers is in verse 28: our redemption is near. John 14:27 says, "Peace I leave with you, My peace I give to you; not as the world gives do I give to you. Let not your heart be troubled, neither let it be afraid"—a grand promise indeed!

CHAPTER 19

1. Answer based on personal experience. Some examples could include Matthew 5:4 and 2 Corinthians 1:3–4.
2. Rowan and Lijah represent the "two witnesses" described in Revelation 11. Their mission is to prophesy (verse 3) and to execute judgment (verses 5–6).
3. Moses and Elijah.

CHAPTER 20

1. Answers will vary.

CHAPTER 21

1. Revelation 11:3 specifies 1,260 days, which is the same as forty-two months or three-and-a-half years.

CHAPTER 22

1. According to Revelation 11:7, the beast (Satan) "will make war against them, overcome them, and kill them."

CHAPTER 23

1. Verse 10 says that they celebrate and send one another gifts.

CHAPTER 24 AND EPILOGUE

1. The Life Spice represents the working of the "spirit of life from God" (the Holy Spirit, KJV) to bring them back to life, described in Revelation 11:11.

2. The Prince says that the days of Lucius and his Shadow Warriors are numbered and that He will return and conquer them. Likewise, Jesus will return with His saints in glory, conquer the beast and the false prophet, and cast them into the lake of fire. Satan will be bound and cast into the bottomless pit for a thousand years.

3. The rest of the story is told in *Kingdom's Reign*.

4. John 14:12 says, "He who believes in Me, the works that I do he will do also; and greater works than these he will do, because I go to My Father." Burn bright for God and watch what He will do!

The Final Call

Written by Emily Elizabeth Black

AUTHOR COMMENTARY

The purpose of *Sir Rowan and the Camerian Conquest* is twofold: first, to explore and reveal the consequences that result from a stronghold of pride, and second, to close out the Knights of Arrethtrae Series with a speculative storyline leading up to the return of Christ by using the prophecy of the two witnesses as foretold in Scripture.

The first sin committed against God, and perhaps the most dangerous, is that of pride. The five "I wills" of Lucifer in Isaiah 14:12–14 testify to the prideful heart that spawned evil in God's creation. Lucifer knew this sin well and used it to tempt Adam and Eve in the garden when he stated that they would be as gods, knowing good and evil.

Perhaps this is why one central theme seems to ring loudly throughout Scripture: God hates pride. Proverbs 6:16–19 succinctly lists the things God hates, and pride is at the top of the list:

These six things doth the LORD hate: yea, seven are an abomination unto him: a proud look, a lying tongue, and hands that shed innocent blood, an heart that deviseth wicked imaginations, feet that be swift in running to mischief, a false witness that speaketh lies, and he that soweth discord among brethren. (KJV)

Additionally, God warns us over and over that pride will bring us to destruction, and this rings true in human experience. In fact, whenever a great Christian man or woman has fallen, pride seems to be the core reason for that fall.

The antithesis of pride, of course, is humility, a quality God encourages us to daily seek. The Bible tells us, "Humble yourselves in the sight of the Lord, and He will lift you up" (James 4:10).

Unfortunately, just as Sir Rowan learned, the consequences of having a prideful heart are often extremely painful and humbling. When a believer has a stronghold of pride, God often must utterly break that person in order for him or her to be restored to a spirit of humility. It is important to daily remember the words of David: "The sacrifices of God are a broken spirit: a broken and a contrite heart, O God, thou wilt not despise" (Psalm 51:17, KJV).

Finally, a spirit of pride can keep us from entering or continuing effective service for the Lord. In fact, Scripture tells us that God "resists" the proud. Only when we humble ourselves before Him, when we acknowledge that we can do nothing in and of ourselves, will the Lord use us to do mighty things through Him for His kingdom.

> But he giveth more grace. Wherefore he saith, God resisteth the proud, but giveth grace unto the humble. (James 4:6, KJV)

The prophecy of the two witnesses in Revelation 11 is one of the most intriguing aspects of the end-time scriptures. The great speculation regarding the interpretation of these passages allows sufficient room for literary freedom in an allegory such as this. I considered it appropriate to tie in this prophecy to the closing book of the Knights of Arrethtrae Series since the theme of the books is to tell of the great deeds of a few of the mighty Knights of the Prince.

The two witnesses, if literally interpreted, will be perhaps two of the most bold and dramatic messengers ever to have lived. Whether literal or symbolic, the advent of the two witnesses will certainly initiate a time of judgment, renewal, and profound prophetic fulfillment. My allegorical depiction of the end times is only one very loose interpretation, and it is not my intention to presume that this is an accurate rendition of the time line of future biblical events. Rather, it is my hope and prayer that it will inspire you to live all the more passionately for Jesus Christ as His return draws close.

> And, behold, I come quickly; and my reward is with me, to give every man according as his work shall be.
>
> —REVELATION 22:12, KJV